A NASCENT JOURNEY

Karen E. Chin

CLMPublishing

Contact the author at:
booksbyjasmine@gmail.com

Published by CLM Publishing.
Cayman Islands.
www.clmpublishing.com

ISBN 978-1-948074-25-4

This title is also available in eBook.

Printed in the United States of America.

DEDICATION

"Denise" — an unlikely
Good Samaritan — thank you.

ONE

*The two most important days in your life are the
day you were born and the day you find out why.*

~ Mark Twain

Claire, the mild-mannered, soft-spoken, third
sibling of eight, has lived a good part of
her life in small villages. Her parents have
moved the family around from one after another;
better dwelling places for us. Each place had turned into
a disappointment in a nightmarish kind of bad, one
after another, but they kept on going, always hoping
the best was yet to come.

Her parents worked hard at making a good life
for the family; in many of the villages they have lived,
some children were not so fortunate. The villagers'
lifestyle was only a step away from catching up with
them and in some instances, overtaking them. It is a
sad but typical reality for many.

It was no surprise that this new village was big on
trouble and twice on corruption. And, to muddy the

pot, it appeared her parents chose the crudest part to settle in.

It wasn't easy, but Claire worked on never being alone on the streets. With seven siblings it shouldn't be hard, but they each had their own *space* to cover.

From a young child to an adolescent, Claire had seen enough violence and multiple shades of corruption that could have turned her into a delinquent, but she worked through the struggles and pressed on to the good side. Many say she's hardened. She likes to think she has to be that way or get swallowed up by the violence and the uninhibited lifestyle. Keeping on the straight path is a choice she made early and continually affirmed it to keep her balance.

Considered a pragmatic person, she refused to be so rosy-eyed that she doesn't see the truth in what is before her. Many think it's not a friendly nature in someone so young, but she thinks it's not a bad thing either. She's never surprised or thinks it strange when observers point out her rationalism. The realist armor served her well; she was in no hurry to be disarmed.

Having gone to both primary and high schools and achieved only a few passes in the educational field, Claire started working as a room attendant, housekeeping department, at a hotel in the city, close to her eighteenth birthday. Working at that age was a norm for the people in the village and her family; her two older siblings both had wage jobs in the handyperson industry by their sixteenth birthdays. Going straight out of high or secondary school on to college was sporadic in her village, and the few families that could afford the *luxury* only had one or two children in the household to consider; not her filled to capacity house.

Fortunately for kids today, scholarships and grants are available that can assist with college tuitions. Do not let your dreams die before they begin! Give yourself that step ahead by taking every opportunity available at hand to further your education.

Every workday, Claire must take two transports to get to work; a taxi from her village into the main town and then a bus into the city. From her village, and most of the country, riding in a taxi means sharing space with five other persons, excluding the driver, and sitting on seats that provide no comfort for the uneven roads. The bus rides, to some extent, were enjoyable; they fed her imagination. But it robbed her of pleasant air and alone time.

On many of her morning rides in to work, Claire had to imagine being chauffeured instead of sitting or standing on an overcrowded bus with people with body odors too *ripe* for that early in the morning. Can you imagine the ride after eight hours on the job? Eek!

The Intercontinental Hotel where Claire worked was part of a hotel chain and was on the waterfront in the downtown part of the city. Being newly built, the beautiful, white-dove-painted rooms were welcoming; there's nothing like the fresh scent of linens and new furniture blended with the sea breeze. Calming.

The wage wasn't great; neither was the position anything to brag about. But it was good enough to provide some necessities for her and to contribute towards the household. Her mom and dad, whenever he was home from farm working, worked freelance jobs; housekeeping and selling ice cream, respectively. They respected the pennies in the house as they were hard earned.

One *superb* thing about the job is that Claire meets people from different countries; some she's interested in and some find her interesting. Being young and not so plain-looking, on her journey to work and different places, she drew attention. At one time she held the attention of a famous footballer from Paraguay. It was exhilarating to know he desired her; that she held his attention. It lifted her confidence and aptitude. However, having trust issues, the devotion wasn't as fruitful or productive as she might have hoped.

Her *rational* thinking persuaded her to believe he was just a lonely guy far from home hoping to get with a *local* gal. Sadly, it was not as she thought. He tried a few times to correct her view; a few of his teammates also *vouched* for him. But the distrust could not be undone. Her little to no interest in a relationship didn't sit well with him and he didn't like what she voiced about him only wanting to *tame his heel* with a local gal. Anyhow, that was that.

That brief encounter opened a little trust; however, the opportunity to be with her Paraguayan never came back around. When he departed to his country, they kept in touch writing each other for a while; no social network and instant messaging then, so the distance and time destroyed the remaining threads of interest. Before he left, it never came up if he was ever coming back to visit her, and there was no invitation for her to come visit him, which made her believe she was right about the *heel* cooling.

Talk about distrust!

His departure closed that chapter of the closest she got to a would-be *foreign* suitor in that stage of her life. Several local *would-be* suitors crossed her path, but her focus was on finding a new form of work, so she gave no notice to their attention.

Her struggles were real; to transition to find something other than cleaning rooms. It's very difficult to get a good-paying job or position without proper education and connection.

Listen carefully, if a path is before you to choose a wage job for instant pay or to go on to college for a career, choose the career path. It may be a bit longer to earning some funds, but you will command your salary and your placement will be easier.

People often tell her she is a pleasant-looking girl with a welcoming and attractive smile, so every new person in her life, Claire chalked up to her ability to make friends easily. She was loved. She naturally drew people to her easygoing nature. She thinks it's a gift and a curse.

She considered it a curse because sometimes some not-so-pleasant people entered her life and stayed around far longer than they should, but she learned to take it in stride. Given time, some of those people continued their journey out of her life and matched up with other people they complemented.

She believed and never lost sight of the fact that we are on this journey where we are for a purpose. It might not be clear in the beginning or while you are walking a path, but if you look back at your journey, you will find there was purpose.

Who knows; maybe the not-so-pleasant people changed Claire to be a little more trusting.

Who knows if she also is a not-so-friendly person in someone else's eye? These reflections refocused her, made a little more observant, and sometimes, a lot more tolerant.

If you haven't figured it out, take note that tolerance is necessary on any journey. You may meet people that will not be your ideal choice of friends or acquaintances, but if you are ever in a bind, hopefully you will come from that more welcoming of all people.

For Claire, the chance to leave home to go to work daily was a holiday, but the work was no vacation. The hours were long. There was hardly time for friends and just hanging out; not that her parents would allow her anyway. Her mom is an avid subscriber to the words, "The devil finds work for idlers," so if you don't want to be employed by the devil, you must be busy with anything but recreational stuff. She reinforces that we should leave no time for *non-essential* things. So, movie nights and beach days were only on the pages of the books in the house.

There were some perks on the job; especially meeting people and paying half price on meals and such. But Claire didn't look forward to working on shifts.

Whenever she worked on the night shifts, it meant getting the late bus and a later taxi into her village. Going to her village in the day is a bad idea, so the night was worse. The other alternative was to stay with relatives in town closer to work, if she worked late. Staying with relatives meant borrowing garments to go to work the day after. Not something she looked forward to. She was too proud, and didn't hide her pride well. Claire didn't like handouts. As a child, she had gotten lots of second and third-wear clothing from her mom's former employers and from her older sister. She didn't want wearing other people's clothes tagged to her through to her adulthood.

Appallingly independent, Claire worked hard making a path for herself; she didn't enjoy being at someone's mercy. So, after two late nights and borrowed clothes, Claire never left home without packing an extra top, for *just in case* moments. She tried to be prepared for everything. She worked on being two steps ahead of anything and anyone; but it didn't always come off as preparation.

Of course, a time came when her preparation was not even close to good enough. It made the hotel room cleaning job like living in Manhattan.

One day, if you haven't already done so, you may discover that your preparedness and plans don't always walk the same pace as you. You may find that as much as you try to be prepared, you are not even close to ready. You may also discover that life's troubles may leave some sliders in your path; you can either slide along or get tripped up.

The choice is always yours.

TWO

The days at work, and the workload itself, could get hectic, so much so that sometimes all that was in her was the strength to get on her mode of transport to get home and straight to bed. But no matter how tired she may feel at the end of a day, the next day would find Claire getting ready to go to work and do it again. The zest to do a well-done job is a driving force in all that she undertakes. And with the limitation on work, she worked hard not to lose her current position.

It appears no matter how hard or out-of-character a job is, a person will try not to lose it. Maybe it is pride. Who would want to put on their resume *fired* from any job?

Over the twelve-month span Claire worked at the hotel, she met people from as far as Europe and Africa and as near as some other countries in the Caribbean. Some people stood out more than others because of how they have affected her life, and sometimes because of where they were from, especially if she had never heard of the country. It fascinated her to learn that there were many countries with remarkable people. She wasn't narrow-minded, but she wasn't aware so many people from different countries knew about her island and loved to visit. Seeing and learning from so many people from different parts of the world made her wonder what she did with her time in Geography and History classes. That learning formed a new obsession; a dream to see as many countries as possible.

Every chance she got, she would go to the library and look up the different countries and talked with the guests to find what their country was like.

It was one of those times she met a guest who was visiting from another island in the Caribbean. The guest's name was Mrs. Carmine Thompson. She worked at a hotel as well; she said she was the front desk supervisor and had worked in the present position and hotel for nearly *twenty years*. A few times in their conversations, Mrs. Thompson said she enjoys her work and meeting people. She also reminded Claire that she had been working at the hotel longer than Claire had been born.

The friendship seemed to develop over the length of Mrs. Thompson's stay. Twice in Mrs. Thompson's ten-day stay, Claire stayed back after work to show her around the town and to help her with minor chores. Her husband was also with her. Claire learned that the Thompsons' visit was for medical reasons and it was hectic for them, so they appreciated Claire's help.

Unlike some people, Mrs. Thompson didn't seem to judge Claire for the room attendant position. In fact, she said frequently that "at least Claire was busy doing something and not just sitting around waiting for a cushy job or husband and babies." Secretly, Claire had the aspiration for the husband and babies, but she wasn't waiting around, and that was for another time.

Before the end of her stay, Mrs. Thompson invited Claire to come and visit her island when she got some time off, which was coming up some months later. She even offered Claire a place to stay; at her home, with her and her family. Claire was excited to have been given the opportunity.

Mrs. Thompson's portrayal of her islands was very expressive; they sounded like something from a fairy tale. It turned out the islands, three of them, were very close to Jamaica. However, until Mrs. Thompson mentioned them, Claire never heard about the Cayman Islands.

She also said the islands were first called Las Tortugas — something to do with turtles — but now are called the Cayman Islands; Grand Cayman, Cayman Brac, and Little Cayman. It's interesting to note that the islands were named after turtles and then renamed after crocodiles. Mrs. Thompson said the word *Cayman* in Spanish is *Caiman*, which means crocodiles.

She said the islands were small; a little over a hundred square miles, with a population of just over 37,000 people. There were no mountains, unlike the many in Claire's country. She said the highest point on the islands was like a huge rock found in Cayman Brac, and they called it the Bluff; lots of people visit it, as it overlooks the sea. The smallest of the islands, Little Cayman, was like a zoo; it had a diverse group of wildlife, from endangered iguanas to many species of birds unique to the island.

Claire's busy mind and overactive imagination traveled to the islands and visited all the places. They intrigued her. So, she vowed she was going to visit someday.

She would take Mrs. Thompson up on her invitation; especially the added part that if she liked the island and was interested in staying longer, Mrs. Thompson would help her get a job at her workplace, as they were looking for pleasant young people such as Claire to work at the front desk or in their novelty stores.

On her departure, Mrs. Thompson thanked Claire for her extra help and reminded her to come and visit when she can; she gave her phone number so they could keep in touch. Claire did.

Seven months later, when it was vacation time, Claire decided to go to Mrs. Thompson's island, Grand Cayman. It would be a tremendous step for her, as she had never even gone to the airport. Her only encounter with airplanes was when they flew high in the sky over her head.

If she got to go on the trip, it would secretly fulfill one of her dreams. She said *if*, as the traveling idea was a difficult subject to talk about. Her parents didn't even like any of the kids talking about camping trips together away from home, much less going abroad alone.

Tentatively voicing her plans first to her parents and then with Mrs. Thompson, she got okays from both sides. It wasn't so simple to get a yes from her parents; they didn't readily agree. But as Claire had talked about Mrs. Thompson with them a while back and had mentioned what she was like, her parents were familiar with the person and the name and gave in, after much persuading and pleading. Mrs. Thompson agreed readily and said she was looking forward to her visit and was excited about her involvement in Claire's first trip abroad.

Fully encouraged, Claire set her focus on planning her trip and putting together every penny she had, along with some from her parents and even the neighbors, to buy her plane ticket for her vacation, and possible job-hunting.

The weeks leading up to the trip, Claire's nerves were on edge; it felt like sleeping on a bed of pins and needles. The trip was an enormous step; the biggest thing she was undertaking, and alone. Aside from Mrs. Thompson, the island would be as isolated and foreign for her as an Alaskan native would be in the desert. Going to Grand Cayman wasn't like she was traveling to visit her grandparents in the country or staying overnight at a relative's. She was going far into the unknown, on a journey.

It would be life-changing; but did she know how extreme it would be?

THREE

"Can you imagine, young Claire is leaving home to go overseas?!"

"Have you seen the state of her parents? They are going out of their minds."

"Anyone know how long she's going for?"

"A who Claire knows a foreign?"

"A which foreign she going, anyway?"

Those were some *talks* in her village.

Everybody wanted a say about her trip; they felt entitled because of their penny investment. She tried to be respectful, especially to those who gave towards her trip, but there were those who added to her parents' worrying by questioning them constantly with *have you met the person she is going to*?

Her mother already had reservations about her going so far away; the villagers weren't making things easier by adding to the pile. The village talked so much about how far she was going to an unknown person; they nearly convinced her parents to cancel the trip.

If it had gotten to the cancellation part, Claire was planning to play the age card. She was over her eighteenth birthday, but before it came to that, her parents had conceded. The *age card* went back in her pocket where it really belonged. Of course, she didn't want to get to that place anyway, because she knew her parents would just flip it on her and ask, "Whose roof you under?" She had heard that sentence before when one of the older siblings was *misbehaving* and played the age card, at twenty-one years old!

The role of her parents seemed never-ending, and Claire believed they'd take it to the extreme. They didn't believe in the age thing. You will always be their children, even when you are married with six children of your own.

Regarding her job at the hotel, her mom wasn't proud of the cleaning position, but she was happy Claire found employment, so that was good news. Her mother wanted more for her. She wanted Claire to become a nurse and even tried to get her to go to nursing school; she had the minimum requirement of Mathematics and English passes in CXC. However, Claire wanted to be a flight attendant (back then they were called Air Hostess). Neither opportunity to be a nurse or a flight attendant presented itself, as money was an issue to further the studies and the trainings needed.

Truth is, Claire never went for the test to become a flight attendant, so how could she get in? Here's a side note: If you never try for something, you will never succeed at it. You can't pass something you never attempt. When you remember that, you will live without regrets and can't blame someone else about your missed opportunity.

Put the work in, if you want to achieve something.

So, now the opportunity had arrived to travel abroad. Claire knew it wasn't just for her; it was for her family and the community. The entire village celebrated her break, even though they feared for her. The farthest she had been from home was to her job in the city, a little over an hour drive on a good no traffic day, and to the country to see her grandparents, a three- to four-hour drive. Though she loved her grandparents, she wasn't too fond of country life, so she didn't stay there for long periods or go there often.

Traveling abroad wasn't new to Claire's house. Her father was a farm worker for the USA sugarcane crops and had traveled nearly all Claire's life. But it was a rarity for any of her siblings or the children in the entire village.

Claire's parents' house, the trendsetter of the village, struck again, she heard someone said.

It is funny, not jovial, to know that the village is quite despicable; arguing, fighting, shooting, and a whole lot more, but they look out for each other. The community celebrated when she got her job at the hotel, so it wasn't strange for them to be a part of her new journey. They were every bit involved in her life, as most of them had been by her house for either one thing or another, at one time or another.

Even if she lived to be one hundred and one, Claire couldn't forget the days leading up to the trip and on the journey to the airport, her parents cautioned her the way one cautions a six-year-old going on a field trip.

"Don't take or carry any package from anyone."

"Don't talk to strangers."

"Don't say you are traveling alone."

"Always monitor your bags."

"Make sure to watch and stay close to the air hostess."

"Don't let anyone hold your things."

"Eat nothing from anyone, unless you get it from the air hostess."

"Watch out for your bags."

"If you are going to the bathroom, take your bags with you." Repeatedly.

And one of Claire's favorite reminders, "Call us when your flight lands at the airport and when you reach the house, no matter how late."

How old was she again? Right, eighteen and some months.

Her parents played round robin on her; they took turns laying out so many dos and don'ts; it was hard to remember who said what. Truth be told, they were on point. How parents think up these scenarios so on the spot is yet to be solved. Her parents drilled into her the importance of keeping a hawk-eye gaze around her.

In those days, in Claire's country, pay phones on the side of the roads were the in thing. All you needed was the phone number and coins. Her parents hoped it was the same on Mrs. Thompson's island, so she could call from the airport.

Anyway, to this day, Claire is happy that her parents went with her to the airport and had drilled in her brain the information of not carrying anything for anyone or leaving her luggage unattended.

When they got to the airport, there were a lot of higglers asking persons to give them luggage space/

weight if you only had one piece of luggage; baggage allowance was two free pieces on the plane and a carryon. If her parents and some villagers weren't with her, she may have caved in, totally ignoring the warning.

There are horror stories today of persons carrying someone else's luggage, including baby products or stuffed animals, out of the goodness of their heart. The regrets are enormous. Some people ended up in jail just for saying yes to what looked like a *desperate* traveler.

Yikes!

Now, here she was, going abroad for the first time, boarding an airplane to the Cayman Islands, where the only person she knew was a lady she'd met briefly while cleaning a hotel room.

Is that not a horror story? Yet to be answered.

After the Kingston airport experience, checking in, waiting on the flight and the airplane ride, three hours and fifty-five minutes later, Claire landed on Grand Cayman, Mrs. Thompson's island. It was well after 8:00 pm. The flight was only fifty-five minutes.

The islands were so close to Jamaica; why hadn't she heard about them or met anyone from there? Maybe they were mentioned before, but they were insignificant to her then. Not anymore. Funny how the mind works.

It was a rough flight; lots of turbulence. Being it was her first flight, she had no experience to compare, but by her estimation and experience, it was rough. There are many flights daily; it couldn't be like that all the time or people wouldn't be traveling so often. Unless they were suckers for pain and motion sickness!

She could not see much of the island from the plane window except for a lot of Christmas lights, the most she had seen in her entire life! They must do Christmas big.

It was a small airport; easy to navigate. So as soon as they processed her Claire made her way outside the building to meet with Mrs. Thompson. They had spoken earlier that morning and set the arrangement where they were to meet. Mrs. Thompson had told her that as soon as she exited the airport, she was to make her way to the end of the walkway immediately outside.

She scanned the crowd, but the familiar face of Mrs. Thompson wasn't among the gathering, neither anyone holding a sign with Claire's name. She was at least expecting, if not Mrs. Thompson, one of her children. She said she had seven of them, and most of them were young adults and teens. Also, she said her husband had five children before their marriage, so there was no lack in receivers.

There were many people happily greeting the ones they were meeting; maybe relatives and friends. There were a lot of cars for such a small airport and the small number of passengers. Additionally, there were taxicabs seeking fares.

Standing on the outside of the lounge, nervous and a little afraid, waiting, Claire walked the conversation she had with Mrs. Thompson earlier through her mind to be certain she missed nothing.

Mrs. Thompson had told her when her flight landed and she cleared immigration, she was to wait on the outside for her. She had described even the very color of the sign at the end of the walkway Claire should stand beside.

She did as she was told, or as far as she understood the instructions. So why was her welcoming party missing?

As the sinking pit in her stomach floated around her, she got even more apprehensive. This shouldn't be the first experience for anyone in a foreign country.

Right now, she would gladly receive a message even by a pigeon.

Looking around at the people moving about, no one seemed concerned about the panicky, wild-eye-looking, fresh-off-the-boat girl. Claire hoped she wasn't looking the way she felt, like a deer caught in the crosshair of a hunter.

She knew a little about the island outside of what she had learned from Mrs. Thompson. She had done a little library visit to learn more about the place and what it was really like. She had felt confident in her initiative to have learned a little above what she had heard, but now that confidence was dissipating. Waiting can rob even a thief of a *learned* craft. It's hard to build confidence in waiting.

She tried consoling herself with the fact that the country wasn't known for *horror* stories of kidnapping or murders, but the ever fickleness of her mind reminded her that there's always a first.

She tried, but with difficulty, to remain patient. She knew how to wait, but she hadn't mastered the patience of it.

Forty-five minutes later and a few calls to the house yielded no response; none. Panic took up a seat in her mind. Fear increased because the handful of remaining people at the airport kept asking if she was okay. Nothing makes you feel more anxious or adds to your anxiety than the dreaded, "Are you okay?" one too many times. Her yes answers were brave, but inside, she was crumbling. Sure, she was being over-cautious not to talk to strangers or let people know more than they needed to, coupled with an all-time high distrust, but where was that leading? Maybe stranded at the airport.

People were leaving her alone at her quick responses of yes. Her sharp and short answer caused others who overheard her not to bother to ask. As time stretched on, she got her wish.

Her parents had cautioned her on everything they thought she needed for the journey. Claire had propped and prepared herself as well. But there were no notes to pull from for being stranded at an airport in a foreign place. She was told, many times, *don't talk to a stranger*.

O-o-o-k-kay.

What now, *Kemosabe*?

FOUR

Claire was experiencing now what her parents tried to teach her: to never leave home alone. Their worst fear for their child had come to collect a payment with dear life. Fear was running through her like blood runs through the vein.

The airport was being emptied. Her opportunities were dwindling by the moment. Only a few passengers and two cab drivers remained, and they didn't seem to be staying longer. Her eyes were stuck on the beacon sign as it flashed before her; *don't talk to stranger*. With no call-a-friend helpline available, and the one friend she knew here missing in action, what does one do in this situation?

She tried not to stare, as it is impolite, but her focus kept going back to one of the taxi drivers, who also had asked several times if she was okay; he was an elderly gentleman. He seemed to have assigned himself as her questioner. He was approaching her again.

When she first got outside the airport, he was sitting in the cab nearest to the door and asked if she needed a cab. She had answered no. He must have left the terminal at some point, as she hadn't seen him for a while.

As he reached her, he asked, "Are you okay?" again, but before she could respond, he told her he had two granddaughters who looked about the same age as Claire and was quite worried to leave her at the airport, as this was his last run for the evening. He continued on to say that there was no other flight for the night, and the workers would leave soon. Therefore, the airport would be closed.

Luckily, or so it appeared, an immigration officer emerged from inside the building. She recalled he was close to where she was processed. Fearful that he would question why she was still at the airport, and when she told him that no one came to pick her up, he would probably send her back on the plane, she turned her attention to the taxi driver. She answered him with a longer response or with more information than her parents would approve to give a stranger; if she could talk to one, that is.

Claire told the taxi driver about her trip to the island being her first time traveling anywhere and that she was waiting to be picked up by the person who invited her. She mentioned how she had met her inviter and the arrangements they made. When she paused for a little, or ran out of other things to share, the driver said he could drop Claire where she wanted to go; what's the address?

Mmm-hmm.

Now why didn't she think of that?

Mind, you have my permission to zap yourself. An address.

Why didn't you think of that?
Who goes anywhere without knowing their destination?
Oh, yeah, pragmatic Claire, who is always prepared.

Mrs. Thompson had given her the phone number and until then, the absentee address wasn't an issue.

Who needs an address when you have a phone number and are in constant contact with the person on the other end? Well, until now.

She didn't even need an address to be landed. In fact, not even the immigration processor had asked for one. Seemingly, just saying the name of the person she was going to stay with was good enough. Maybe they had Mrs. Thompson's address in their system; it is, after all, the chief port of entry. Maybe the Cayman Islands is to tiny; but the lack of address now proved not small enough.

You foolish, foolish girl, Claire admonished herself.

It was hard to suppress the nauseating feeling in her stomach. What had she gotten herself into?

Though inwardly reprimanding herself on her *country-bumpkin,*[1] sheltered, no-thinking lifestyle, Claire apologized to the driver she didn't have an address, only the phone number of her inviter. Well, that revelation started a whole other conversation on what Claire should or shouldn't do, on safety, and on the importance of "this" and "that." What was she thinking, coming to a place for the first time with only a phone number? He laid it out there. Her ears were singing as if he engraved his list on her head.

---

[1] A naïve or unsophisticated person.

She thought she left her father back home.

Guess it doesn't matter where you are; it seemed a village still raises a child.

He tried to help her by formulating a list of questions he thought would help narrow down the address. But Claire's mind went independent and jeered her with, *What does he expect? You weren't even smart enough to collect an address.*

She still hadn't mentioned Mrs. Thompson's name. It was bad enough she had to *talk to a stranger;* it didn't mean she had to share everything. But she was getting close to letting her name out; she needed the help, and she would not let it pass her.

Maybe telling him her name would stop him from filling her with so much tourist guide information; he was relaying the info the same way some people recite the Lord's Prayer.

According to the driver, he knew the entire island; from east to west and north to south. His profession as a taxi driver should have given her the hint.

Feeling worn-out, Claire told him she was going to a Mrs. Thompson, which led him to ask more questions. What is Mrs. Thompson's first name? Did Claire know any other relative of Mrs. Thompson? Where does Mrs. Thompson work? And if she remembered anything special about Mrs. Thompson; a mark, accent, young, old...

He must have been a private investigator in a former life. His questions and her subsequent answers led him to exactly who Claire was talking about. He said being a small island, everyone knew everyone. Why didn't he say that in the beginning? They could have saved themselves a good thirty questions and several minutes.

But it was true; he knew Mrs. Thompson. Soon, he named all Mrs. Thompson's children and her husband and his *outside* children as well. He even named the school-age children's schools, the helper, and the pet. The man was a walking databank on all things Thompson! "But, regrettably," he said, lowering his voice as if sharing a trade secret, or to ease the shock of the bomb about to be dropped, "I took the Thompsons here earlier today for a flight for the United States of America!"

Chorus time: "Say waaah!?"

As a driver, he probably takes many people to and from the airport, so he might be confused about the *fare*. There could be a lot of Thompsons, for all she knew.

It was an unquestionable fact he was mistaken.

He was definitely, most infinitely wrong!

Okay, Claire, saying it twice won't change the answer. You just named the man a databank. You can't shoot the messenger. He may be your only ride to wherever.

It couldn't be the same Mrs. Thompson, she reasoned, and insisted.

Mrs. Thompson had sounded overjoyed this morning when they spoke. It couldn't be the same Mrs. Thompson she spoke with earlier in the day and who even reiterated, "You are welcome anytime." Being here tonight wasn't a last-minute trip; this was planned, months ago.

Mister Driver, you don't know everyone! she wanted to shout, but *respect your elders* swam before her eyes like a banner on a busy highway.

Claire swallowed her words and pushed past the dryness in her throat. Several swallowing attempts got her in a more breathable mode as she tried to look unaffected by the news. But to the eyes of the beholder, she failed miserably. She was well past panicking. It bowled her over and she couldn't do anything about it.

Even her mind was siding with the other side; strike one.

Claire replayed the conversation of that morning with Mrs. Thompson. There was no mention or recollection of Mrs. Thompson's intended departure.

If she had plans for today, Mrs. Thompson could have told her to postpone her trip. It would have been hard and disappointing, but she would have understood. After all, this was a strange place for her, so she would have waited for the person who knew the place to be available. They spoke about the trip many times. At what point did Mrs. Thompson forget that she would not be around to receive Claire? At what point did she forget to say there was no abiding room in the inn for her?

The driver was still waiting on a response, but she was too busy processing her thoughts. Mrs. Thompson's departure today, of all days, wasn't something she'd factored into her plan. She wouldn't have thought about that angle; it never occurred to her.

There's no outward appearance that you can flag some people as not-so-nice. You must take some things in stride and learn from it. Mrs. Thompson didn't strike her as a person who would do such a thing, especially to *sweet* Claire.

Is it sensible to expect nothing from a stranger? Perhaps. But it's even more stupid to expect something from a friend, and get nothing.

Life has a way of teaching you that where you expect help from is not where it will come from. She didn't want that lesson today. She couldn't handle that lesson today. She needed help to come from exactly where she was expecting it; she had no other plan. Not even a backup or spare plan. She was too far from home to call for a pickup.

Realizing that the driver was still waiting, Claire ignored what he presented and adamantly said, "You are mistaken. It can't be the same Mrs. Thompson. We spoke this morning, and she knew I was coming today."

But there was no convincing the driver otherwise. He held fast to what he knew.

She was given another curve ball.

Strike two.

He described the dates the Thompsons took a trip to Jamaica; he was the one who dropped them off and picked them up from the airport for that trip as well. He was correct that the trip was a doctor's visit for Mr. Thompson. And being the source of all information Thompson, the driver knew for a fact that the Thompson children were home and he could drop Claire there.

Strike three.

Was she given the boot before she landed on the island? Was there a sign she missed somewhere? Her first night in and everything she planned or was hoping to happen was going counterclockwise. Can you imagine the children were home, yet no one picked up the call?

Maybe they were told not to pick up *unknown numbers*, she reasoned.

Claire felt the universe was conspiring against her, but she didn't want to believe it.

Whatever you need to tell yourself during a terrible time will make swallowing disappointments easier. Experiencing fear, disappointment, and panic on the same day can quickly lead to depression. So she fought her mind to stay sane.

She thought she had met an authentic Mrs. Thompson who wanted the best for her. Was she that gullible and wanted to reach a foreign land so badly that she accepted without question? She refused to accept that chink in her armor.

She wasn't concerned that her distrust surfaced.

If she was to accept what the driver said, Mrs. Thompson misled her. Probably she wasn't inviting Claire to come, she was just being *nice.* She said the things people like to say, "Come by anytime."

Maybe the driver was up to something as well, feeding her those lies.

He must have seen something on her face as he tried to authenticate who he was and what he was saying. So, he called an immigration officer that was leaving the building to come over. He called the officer by name. The driver told him to tell Claire who he, the driver, was; his name and any related information. He also told the officer that Claire was worried about leaving the airport with him, so if it's not too much trouble, could he note who Claire left with.

That sounded like a good plan; she was low on options.

The officer confirmed who the driver was and added Claire's information and the driver's name, Mr. Bailey, and the cab number, to a notebook he was carrying.

Win-win.

That was the ultimate conviction she needed.

So, after seeing her luggage stored in the car's trunk, Claire took a seat in the taxi. The driver took his seat as well and started up the vehicle, and they set out. She watched as the lights of the airport faded to nothingness, taking with it the only place she now knew on the island.

The foreboding thought *Mama didn't say there would be days like this* played on repeat in her head.

Resigning her mind to her situation, Claire slumped in the seat as she rode into the unknown with a *stranger*.

FIVE

A good plan is to always have a plan. If it's not a quote, it should be.

The airport and the misadventures made it obvious; Claire was plan-less.

As the events of the night played out, she decided to never be on either the receiving or the giving end of such a situation. No one, young or old, regardless of race or creed, male or female, should be placed in such an exposed and helpless environment, deliberate or not.

We are told to choose the road before us and walk carefully on it, but sometimes others choose a road for us and that may be what gets us in calamitous situations. No one can really say whether or not it will be a dangerous road at the beginning of a journey; you have to experience it to know. But we can rely on our instincts or sixth sense or the Holy Spirit, if active in our lives, to help us make wise decisions even midway. Have faith as a life raft or you will sink.

Claire was excited about her trip and meeting up with Mrs. Thompson again. She wanted to see some of the island.

She hadn't known Mrs. Thompson long; seven and a half months ago when she was at the hotel. They talked occasionally in between, and Claire found her to be motherly, someone trusting. Nothing had caused her to think otherwise.

Aside from the Kingston airport experience with the higglers when her parents rescued her, and getting to travel to the island, Claire was grateful for her parents' insistence on giving her what they called *emergency* funds. Her mother had said, "Always carry your taxi fare wherever you go, even if it is on a trip in your best friend's car. Things happen." And it can get to "things happen" quickly, even when you are prepared.

The emergency fund was small, but with no one to pick her up from the airport, she had to dip into it for cab fare. Though the driver was sympathetic of her predicament, he made no mention it was going to be a free ride. In fact, at the onset of the journey, he had said it didn't cost a lot to get to the Thompsons. So, Claire shouldn't have to wait on the ride. That hint of *it doesn't cost a lot* should clue her in. It wasn't a free ride.

Nevertheless, what does he consider not a lot of money? Does Mister Source of Information know that a penny is a lot if that's all you've got?

Anyhow, if the airport no-ride was anything to go by, what else was there? Would this mean she would need to cover a place to stay?

Calling all pennies near and far. Come in!

This is not a drill. Emergency dispatch to Claire.

The drive to Mrs. Thompson's house took less than fifteen minutes, but it felt like hours as the driver kept up a hearty conversation about the island and the people. Claire's mind went on a downward spiral of hopelessness. She thought he had said all there was about the island back before she got into the cab; apparently not.

Seemed part of his duty was to entertain his fares, and she had to admit he did the job well. On any other night, possibly one where she wasn't in mortal danger, she would have *enjoyed* the verbose regality on the island. It was an excellent knowledge to have. But on a night like tonight, when he was trying to feed her so much, it wasn't welcoming.

Hey, mister, it is night, after all. Save something for the light of day.

But he didn't cease talking. He talked about the islands' settlers; where to eat, what to do, and how to move around. From what he said, it was best to stay in a certain area if she planned to be around long. It wasn't because of any crime or bad issues why she was *warned,* but as the gentleman said, "You can never get in a problem if you know your place." His exact words.

It was a pity she didn't ask what *place*.

She wasn't familiar with segregation on any scale, racial equality, or poverty, but it wears you down when you must know your place.

She hoped she wouldn't regret not knowing.

Maybe her place was to have stayed in her cozy family nest back in Jamaica.

After seeing her safely to the gate of what he called the Thompsons' house, and receiving her big thank you and the exact fare, Mr. Bailey went on his way, cheerfully humming a tune.

Who could hum in this dark? Must be to chase ghosts away. Maybe he felt pleased that he rescued her from would-be predators. She wished she could have given him a little extra for being such a great help, but the funds were extremely limited. Even a penny was too much to think to give away. She knew the maxim, "You have to give to receive," but she closed her hands tightly on the pennies.

Tonight, it was best to be a miser.

As she watched him reverse the car from the lane and turn onto the main street, his car headlights vanished and took with them the surety of the second person known to her on this island.

Well, that's that.

Leaving the airport parking lot took away the opportunity of going backward; she wasn't interested, anyway. The only way now was forward.

She resigned her mind to accept the journey that brought her to this porch; all she needed now was to see Mrs. Thompson. It would be just as if she had come to the airport. She was desperately hoping that the driver was wrong about her departure to the USA.

Standing on the porch of what Mr. Bailey called the Thompsons' place, she took a deep breath, tried composing her trembling hand, and then knocked on the door. It took several knocks and some talking through the closed door to get someone to open it.

Pleasantries prepared, the face-to-face "good evening" got stuck on Claire's lip as a fair-skinned young girl, about Claire's age, greeted her. However, her face lacked the trademark smile of greeting someone. Perhaps it was the hour in the night. Perchance Claire disturbed her sleep or reading time. Hopefully, it was a wonderful book.

"Can I help you?" the young girl said. The greeting seemed void of emotion.

"Good evening. My name is Claire Sims. Can I speak with Mrs. Thompson?"

There was still no welcoming smile or recognition after Claire gave her name.

Peradventure she wasn't at the right place.

"Mrs. Thompson isn't here right now. What is it regarding?"

Yep, definitely the right place.

Inhaling deeply, Claire said, "I am from Jamaica. I just arrived on the island. Mrs. Thompson invited me to visit, and she knew I was coming tonight."

"I'm Lisa. My mother left for Miami, Florida, earlier today and said nothing about anyone visiting."

"How can that be? We spoke this morning. She knew I was coming," Claire said imploringly, barely keeping back the tears.

"She has said nothing regarding you or that I should expect someone, so I can't let you inside."

"Please. Can you call her?"

"She left today. We don't have a number to reach her yet. She won't be in touch until tomorrow. There is nothing I can do." She sounded irritated.

End of conversation, it seemed. But she stood there at the half-opened door.

Silence.

Then, deep sighs.

Though the face in front of her showed little to no compassion, Claire tried one last attempt. She couldn't hold back the tears running down her cheeks, but that didn't work either. Lost cause. To add salt to her already opened wound, the girl grumbled something about *the nerve of some people turning up on your doorstep, unannounced and —* Maybe she realized that her grumbling was louder than intended. She stopped mid-sentence, made an impatient shuffle, then gave an apology. But no sooner had she apologized when took away the half-opened door opportunity and closed it, and turned out the porch light.

Double dismissals.

It took a while for it to sink in.

Did that just happen for real?

Pulling what little dignity left in her spine, Claire backed away from the porch on legs of steel and slowly made her way towards the gate. If it was a locked gate, she would count it as triple dismissal. But thankfully, it was just an open space between two walls facing each other; a promise of a future gate. There, she put her suitcase down, which felt loaded with cement blocks, and sat dejectedly on it.

Did that just really happen?

Maybe it was just a nightmarish dream before her trip. She didn't waste time pinching herself; the pain inside was already too much to be unreal.

In a daze, Claire stared at nothing in the dimly lit lane as she tried not to think about her current state. Pleading to no one or nothing, she looked to the open skies. Tears poured out like a broken dam down her face.

It's true; a bad day can easily get worse, Claire discovered. There were toads chirping, and the mosquitos gave her a warm welcome to the island as they serenaded her. Fortunately, they weren't interested in biting, it seemed, and soon got disinterested or got swept away by the light night breeze. With no option, it seemed the outdoors would be her room; the breeze was her fan and the stars her night-lights.

Mr. Bailey's nonstop chatting had long since left. What she wouldn't do to be seated in his cab right now. His constant babbling wasn't so bad after all.

She knew no one except Mrs. Thompson, if that counted. She had nowhere to go. Until Mr. Bailey brought her here, she didn't even know Mrs. Thompson's address. She had no number for a taxi service. And no one else to call.

In one night, in a strange land, her life raft sank. She had gone from a mama-baby country-girl to a not-sure-where-the-next-road-leads homeless person.

As if she couldn't be more embarrassed, it was infuriating as she felt the person or persons in the house watching her.

Going on thirty minutes later, they still did not invite her inside, and Claire did not move from the gate. She was glad they didn't call the authorities either.

She never felt a need to worry about blood pressure, but she wouldn't want to be tested right now; it felt it would read through the roof.

Her sheltered life was no match for this journey.

The gate or outdoors was no place for a young girl—or anyone, for that matter—at night, but she decided she would sit there for as long as it took to survive the night or get help.

Like a biography movie on slow playback speed, Claire reviewed her predicament; at the gate, her journey from the airport, and from her parents' house. Nothing she envisioned from the planning of the trip to the flight painted any picture of her sitting outside like a vagrant.

There was not even a stranger to ask for help. She could do nothing. And that's what she saw in front of her; a vast, dark nothingness. A voided future.

She thought of her shared room with her siblings back home, and though it wasn't something she looked forward to—everyone was practically in everyone's face—it was a pleasant thought tonight. Huddling between so many brothers and sisters wasn't such a bad thing after all; there was a roof over her head and a place to sleep, and though they had little, there would be something to eat. She was starving, but the crucial thing overloading her mind was a safe place to stay.

She thought of herself in the reverse role of the person behind her on the other side of the door and what she would have done for the young stranger at the gate. She hoped she would have acted differently. Lessons are there to be learned in every situation, and she hoped she didn't miss this one, regardless of the state she found herself in.

Trying to forget her dilemma, Claire's mind roamed the stars. It wasn't a horrible night, but being a stranger on the island and in this lane was enough to add clouds of darkness on her path. Every insect behaved like Satan let loose, raining hell's woes on her.

What landed her on this pathway, alone and very much afraid?

She was told she was a lovable, approachable, and easy-to-get-along-with person. Where is that girl tonight? Where are those people who think so? Who will show her compassion? Any Samaritan will do; even a bad one.

As the night got darker, it was getting harder to keep her mind on the positive side. The idea of walking to a few doors in the lane and ask for help or a room for the night crossed her mind, but she stayed seated in terror. The thought of knocking on the wrong door was scarier. If someone said *yes, she could stay.* What guarantee had she of making it back out of that house? Scaring herself with those thoughts kept her planted like a walnut tree where she was.

Searching her mind for a solution, walking back to the airport came up.

It didn't seem like a long drive, so it may be walkable. Maybe the walk would hurry the night; no sense in prolonging a dreadful one. The streets were well lit, so there should be no problem finding her way. The driver had turned only three times on the drive from the airport to the house, and he made two of those turns near the house. But then again, the thought of being *caught* by immigration and sent home grounded her at the spot.

Her mind busied itself with many other thoughts, none helpful to her situation.

She never thought it was possible, but at one point she found that her tear ducts had dried up. She was crying tearlessly, and her humiliation increased as she felt watched. Maybe they would be moved to let her in, even for the night; so, she held her ground. A better way to word it: her fear caused her to stay put.

They may hope she would go away from the gate, but her fear was stronger than their gazes. Let them stare until daybreak; she needed the company anyway.

She tried to encourage herself with something she heard in a church service some time ago: "Even when something bad happens to you, God is still in control." It wasn't helping much, as it didn't seem that way, but she hit replay in her mind to distract herself from what was going on around her.

At least there was something to be thankful for; there was no male that she could see around that knew of her situation. So, no temptation to stay the night with a guy just for the sake of not being homeless. A situation like that could get worse quickly.

Though it was not a happy thought, right now, the only change in her condition was the cramps in her legs and the tightness in her back, but she was thankful.

Either this was the longest day recorded, or being outdoors messed with her track of time. She was living several days in one night at the gate!

SIX

Though she didn't have a watch, she was sure more than an hour had passed, but her situation remained the same. They say, "A mind is a terrible thing to waste," but they never tell you that your mind could waste you away. There were no lacking negative thoughts. And even the positive thoughts agreed with the negatives; *this won't end well*.

No amount of singing, pleading, or praying was working. She was still in the same position, with no help in sight, and the people in the house seemed to have put an invisible door on the porch; her steps refused to take her there to sit for safety. The gate was the only welcoming part of the Thompsons' yard.

Some time later; maybe half an hour or three hours—she didn't give a hoot, as she'd lost interest in time—a mature woman of medium build, wearing what is symbolic of nurses' scrubs appeared in her vision. She *interrupted Claire's company, thoughts, and tearless crying*. Within speaking distance, the woman asked what Claire was doing sitting on a suitcase at the gate. Claire related her story for the third time that night. She told her she came to visit Mrs. Thompson, and that the person who answered the door wouldn't let her in the house, to which the lady gave her the *Mrs. Thompson is away in Miami* story. It looked as if everyone knew Mrs. Thompson would be away, except Claire and Mrs. Thompson.

The lady *chatted* with, or a better word, *questioned,* Claire; who Claire was, where she was from, if she had family or friends on the island, what was her plan.

Would she be sitting in the dead of night, at a stranger's gate, on her suitcase, if there was such a thing as friends and family on the island? She vehemently thought, no way! Even if she had a falling out with her family, she would have chanced it at their gate. They would at least, she hoped, activate the "let not the sun go down on your wrath" Scripture and let her in.

Now, you would think a *motherly figured*-woman, wearing what looked like a nurse's uniform, asking so many personal questions, would take pity on Claire and help her find somewhere, even if it meant staying with her for the night.

Keep thinking.

It didn't work that way.

She pried Claire for more answers and gave her the *nine-yard* whipping about coming to a strange place at night knowing no one.

Not knowing anyone! Didn't she just say she knows Mrs. Thompson? She invited her.

The woman ignored Claire's teary-sounding woes and poured more on her. It appears people *fake care* just to know your business; that's about it.

How much more of my business would you like to know? I got all night.

Nurse lay it on heavily. Considering her situation, she might have done the same to the *idiot* who forgot to know more than one person in a strange land.

Nurse said she rented an apartment in the back of the Thompsons' house and there are other apartments, both occupied and unoccupied, around there. According to Nurse, "If the girl that opened the door didn't want to put you up in the main house, she could put you in one of the rooms in the back."

Sounded like a brilliant plan!

After rambling on about other things, *Mother Nurse* left Claire with a cheery *hope it all works out.* Claire replied, *"Oh, sure, it will all work out. Thanks for helping,"* in the sweetest and purest sarcastic tone her tired tongue could muster, but it was lost on her; she continued on her journey to her *cozy* room in the back.

You know, this should be a quote: *The people you expect to help you are not expecting that of themselves.*

Helping someone is not a DNA thing; it's a humane thing. You must consider what you would have liked done for you and then do it for others. If you want to be helped, you help.

Anyway, if nothing else, at least the woman provided some useful information about the spare rooms in the back. Equipped with the new lead, Claire swallowed her pride a third time and went again to knock on the door, but it was to no avail. The dwellers must have either gone off to sleep in a do-not-disturb, sound-proofed room, or Claire was knocking only in her mind.

Disconsolate, she went back to her post of security guard and gatekeeper.

Now, before you wonder why Claire didn't rent one of those rooms behind Mrs. Thompson's house, you might as well keep wondering. However, the shame-free reason is her pennies refused to come together for the greater good of a rented room, and no one came to the door the second or third time she knocked, so that closed that door, literally.

Not getting into one of the rooms was something Claire thought about later, when she finally had a roof over her head, in a most precarious situation. But if you were retelling this story, stick to, "The emergency fund couldn't live past the operating room."

The whole incident taught Claire a sobering thought she hoped not to forget: whatever is going on in your life, your story might not be as bad as you think. Just because your last hope seemed to have gone out the door, try to hold on, it might just be the breaking of a new day.

After striking out on getting someone to come to the door, and seated in the same way she was before, she picked back up the crying and pleading with God, and really anyone that was on duty in the universe that night.

She busied herself with a new task; given that her working positions had changed to storyteller and security guard, she mentally updated her resume.

She tried to remain alert, but fear fed her every conceivable scenario of homeless, powerless, and loneliness. Honestly, you need little help to fill up on fear when you have yourself as company! In one instant, the mind can be as clear as crystal, bringing good thoughts to your rescue, and the next as crafty as a snake, plotting your own demise. If you don't rein it in, you will carry it through. Be careful not to give your mind lethal information; give it beautiful things to think about.

Just when she succeeded at resigning her mind to her situation and built a wall of fear around her, another lady popped up on the scene. And yes, she wasn't an illusion of imagination. This lady also had an apartment in the back. Evidently, the Thompson place was a popular lodging spot. It also appeared that the tenants were more willing to talk than the main house occupants.

Claire couldn't recall Mrs. Thompson saying anything about rented rooms. Of course it was her private affair, what she owns or doesn't.

Did Mrs. Thompson want Claire to come here as a tenant? Perhaps if she had told Claire she needed to pay rent, maybe she would still be home in Jamaica. But that topic never came up. Here she was, sitting on her suitcase at the gate. Would they charge her rent for here? They could win in court because she was technically on their property.

If this was meant to be a tenant and landlord invitation, Claire's over-glad heart and her penny-short naïve mind didn't recognize the rental clause.

It bears repeating. What had she gotten into?

Somebody's got some explaining to do.

As the lady drew near, she greeted Claire with, "Little girl, why are you sitting out here? Are you crying?"

Maybe darkness gave the impression that Claire was a little girl. She was told that she looked younger than her age, but it wasn't something she placed much salt on. As the years rolled on and she had to produce identification to confirm such, she became a believer. And was sticking with that *little girl* look.

Repeating her story felt like living out the *One Thousand and One Nights* (Arabian nights) tales. Aside from the ache in her stomach, Claire was numb to the pain of her situation. She was getting better at telling the story, as it was scorched on her brain and it was the truth. She has learned that it's easier and better to tell the truth, especially when your life depends on it. So, she felt unburdened relating why she was outside by the gate sitting on her suitcase.

She only hoped that this lady stayed long enough with her to pass some hours. She could do with the company.

No surprise; this lady also knew about Mrs. Thompson being away. She also did some questioning. The questions ran along the same line as the first woman. When Claire responded no to the question of anyone on the island, this lady offered some sympathy. And on top of that, she also offered an opportunity Claire was too afraid not to consider and too practical to refuse, even if it was from a stranger in the middle of the night.

She would be an idiot to even let the offer be withdrawn.

SEVEN

Denise, as Claire learned her name later, wasn't keen on leaving *a young girl outside while she goes to her warm bed*. Her words. She said that her grandmother would whip her and never forgive her, even if she lived to be ninety. So, Claire accepted her offer to go with her to a *safe* place. She said it would be much safer than sitting at the gate. Not that Claire needed much persuading. She had already resigned her mind to accept anywhere but the gate.

But the weirdest thing, Denise's safer place wasn't in the room in the back of Mrs. Thompson's place. Creepy? Yes, but Claire took the offer.

She was in too bad a situation to have a choice. And she didn't question Denise about staying with her in her room in the back of the house.

Living in desperation is not a good, descriptive word to live by; it lowers your integrity or moral compass.

When Denise offered Claire a place to stay, which would be in a second room that she *used occasionally* some streets over from the Thompsons', she saw the red flags waving all over the proposal, but Claire wasn't in a good place to *block the wind.*

All Denise said was if Claire wanted to stay there, she could have it.

If she wanted to stay! What, did she not see that her only offer was the gatekeeping position? Even if you are an axe-murderer — well, the night is still young, so we shall leave that thought in the back of the evidence locker.

Just know, you don't have to offer the room twice.

Claire's desperation took over the conversation and said, "Yes, thank you, I want the room. It's okay by me."

She didn't waste time asking if there was a catch. Even if she had trust issues, rationality overruled. Accepting help from a stranger, going with a stranger, talking to strangers; in one night, she broke all her parents' stranger rules.

You could classify the developments that followed as jumping from the diving board and then learning to swim on the way to the water.

Unknowingly, Claire was enlisted in the school of hard knocks, a course she didn't know existed until her visit to the little island. Just to make it clear, she was an unwilling participant. She was in a classroom picked by the second-greatest teacher — life — and she had no course material to study what they thrust on her. But like an eager student checking off an accomplishments list, Claire placed Mrs. Thompson's airport no-show and no room in her house ordeal and the taxi ride behind her. Soon, because of Denise's offer, homelessness would follow.

In one night, she'd sat for several tests. But, on the flip side, she now knew four persons here on the island; two new ladies, the taxi driver, and Mrs. Thompson. Her friends' circle was improving.

Walking through her working life, it may have started out as a cleaner of hotel rooms, which connected her to a lady from another island. However, that wasn't the big picture. Coming to a country of over 37,000 people, where she knew only one person, wasn't the big picture. The driver that picked her up at the airport and had taken her to a place he thought Claire would be safe, wasn't the bigger picture. Even the youngsters behind the closed door added another layer to her lesson, but they too may have just been part of the framework. The meeting with the two ladies, the unknown nurse lady and Denise, put her on a corrected course and if she stayed focused, she would get to a bigger picture.

The way you go through a challenge helps you go through life. When you connect the difficulties you have faced and overcome with what is facing you now, you will have the strength to live through your next *valley* experience better.

As they stood by the gate talking about the second room, Claire tried to believe the room wasn't a prank or would lead to her doom. She hoped the occupants inside the house were still watching and were feeling terrible. She didn't wish bad for others, but she was hoping, for once, the losing team saw her victory.

Even though they hadn't left the gate, inwardly, Claire was celebrating.

As Denise shared more information about the room, sight unseen, Claire was satisfied it wasn't a sham.

Soon, they both left Mrs. Thompson's gate, on foot, for Claire's new home.

It was a simple walk to get there.

Denise helped carry her bags and entertained and cautioned her, again, with some dos and don'ts of the island. Claire mentally wrote a memo to herself to check why so many people were feeding her all these dos and don'ts. Her parents gave theirs in the day, of which Claire had already broken many. Mr. Bailey gave his list earlier, and now Denise, another stranger, repeated some of what the driver had said, but she also offered some *streetwise* thoughts. To be honest, Denise's animated talk was a welcome distraction. Before long, she had forgotten the ordeal of being unclaimed at the airport, sitting at the gate like a vagrant, and her tearless cries and hunger.

Later, she reflected on many things that ordinarily she wouldn't even consider. She accepted help from strangers, got into a car with someone who had taken her to a place she knew not, and allowed someone else to carry her bags. She was *batting* everything straight out of the park tonight. But given the situation, even a blind referee could see every action was warranted; it was the best plan, as plans went for her.

After listening to Denise's dos and don'ts, she had to agree; they were essential to be adhered to. Also, Denise sounded just like her mom. She could put the fear of hell in the devil while adding frost to the snowman.

It'd been so long since she ate, it was hard to ignore her rumbling stomach; one too many meals missed. Her stomach wasn't keeping quiet about that.

Gosh. They fed her mind with this and that. What about the stomach?

Though the stars were out in their numbers, the location of the room was eerily dark, and it got darker as Denise repeated her long list of what Claire should and shouldn't do. And to strengthen her point, she mentioned what could happen if Claire didn't follow the instructions.

Instructions, huh? That's what you are calling them? Sounds more like boot camp.

Denise's instructions read something like:

- The island is safe, but still practice common sense.
- You are young and beautiful, so keep your ears and eyes open, your legs and mouth closed, and your wits sharp.
- Don't be so eager to leave your parents' home that you land in unpleasant situations.
- Watch out for sweet-talkers.
- Don't talk to or trust strangers.
- Find good examples to emulate.
- Don't take it for granted that only men will harm you."

O-k-a-ay. Is that a hint of something? Should I be worried?

- Change the sheets before you lie in the bed. The room isn't sanitized.

- There's no electricity, so you will need to light the lamp on the table, and be sure to put it out before you fall asleep.
- If you hear knocking on the door, don't open it. I won't be back until morning light.
- Be sensible and alert.
- Notice everything around you, but don't comment on everything you see.
- Say your prayers.

"You know," she said, "I am thankful I am the one that found you. I can't imagine what would have happened otherwise. I have three children; two girls in their teens, like you, and I wouldn't want them to be stranded in any situation anywhere.

"Above all, if I haven't said it, don't talk to strangers, and don't open the door."

Really. You're telling me not to talk to a stranger! And who might you be?

There were a lot more, but geezum, no one could ever fault Claire for a verbatim memory. And she was stuck on thinking Denise didn't look old enough to have daughters Claire's age. Maybe Denise mistook her age; lots of people did.

If she had a choice, the room wasn't anything Claire would have chosen, but she was in no condition to comment on a gift. And what does comfort have to do with anything? The important thing was, it beat homelessness.

She was still thinking through some of Denise's *instructions* and wondered if she was ever going to live past this night and the issues it brought. She hoped with all her heart she would.

No matter what happens tonight, live, Claire, live.

After Denise's departure, Claire locked the door, but within minutes there was a knock. She reached for the handle to open it, thinking Denise came back, but then hesitated as she recalled the warning about not opening the door, and waited. She was hungry. And there was no provision in the room; she checked, so maybe, just maybe, Denise came back with a quick meal for her.

In excitement and partly anxiety to travel, she had ignored the flight attendant's invitation to try some snacks. Now hunger pangs were here to collect. Any food was welcome; she wasn't concerned what it was, and was far from picky who brought it. However, good sense ruled both her hands to keep from unlocking the door and then ruled her stomach.

It is best to be hungry and alive than belly full and dead! kept playing in her head.

Come on! That's worth a Pulitzer or Nobel Prize.

The knocks continued, but as no one spoke, Claire left the door bolted and reinforced it with a chair as a barricade.

She was learning to act sensibly. She made a start.

Early into the morning, there were a lot of knocks. Sometimes different male voices whispered and some shouted.

"Denise. Are you in there?"

"Hey there, are you inside?"

"Denise! Why don't you answer?"

"Denise, open the door!"

"Denise, it's Tony [James] [Paul]!"

"Heck! What's going on?"

Some foul language shared each knocker's frustration.

Though it felt like one of the longest nights for Claire, it was one of the closest she'd walked or talked with God since accepting him as her Lord and Savior five years earlier. Hungry, alone, and very much in fear, Claire read her Bible and cried more tearless tears through the night. One of her comforts was the closed door. The other was focusing on reading Psalm 91; the chapter had never seemed so real. It was as if she couldn't hear anything except the "noisome pestilence" at the door; they wouldn't stop knocking. Though the Scripture offered some comforts, with each knock, fear mounted.

She consoled herself with *at least her spirit was being fed*. She had to read with a dimmed light to give the illusion of no one inside, so she couldn't see much, but it was worth it. Anything to calm the storm raging within her — and to forget the hunger.

She hardly slept.

It seemed morning took its time coming around, but she had never looked forward more to a new day.

Only a day ago she was at home squabbling with her siblings. The squabble amongst the siblings were about who gets the end space in the bed, drawer space for clothes, and her space on the sofa which she had carved out in front of the TV.

Then she was stranded at an airport, followed by being homeless, and then left in a strange room with more suitors knocking than she cared to know about. She welcomed the morning with thanks.

So much can change in twenty-four hours. A person could live a thousand years or a thousand deaths, depending on how one handles fear.

She felt assured she wasn't alone by her time spent talking with God, but fear was present and quenched all possible positive thoughts.

Fear also kept the door locked until Denise came to see her; it was well after 9:00 a.m. She was sure if it had taken Denise the entire day to pass by, she would have stayed behind the closed door. She was hurt, frustrated, disappointed, and sleepy, but she got the chance to stay in an enclosed room. She had to be grateful.

After inquiring on how she was doing and if she had gotten any rest, Denise invited her to go into the town area to get some food and look around. The *look around* idea sounded interesting, as Claire's pennies weren't to be parted with yet, especially on something as *trivial* as breakfast. She tried to back out of going, but it seemed Denise was on a mission; food, and to refuse any no answer from Claire.

There was no bathroom inside the room, so Claire made do with a basin she found under the bed and a bucket of water that Denise mentioned was in the corner for *tidying up* purposes and emergencies; both requirements Claire was fulfilling. The lack of indoor plumbing wasn't Claire's idea of *foreign* life; not how she dreamed it to be. Not that she left a cushy bathroom or lifestyle back home, but there was more convenience. However, she was reminded to be thankful.

Claire finished tidying up and went outside to meet up with Denise, whom she discovered wasn't alone; there were three other ladies waiting with her. The ladies knew of Claire's story and were just as disapproving of the way her visit to the island turned out and her dilemma. They weren't being harsh, just motherly, so it was okay. She needed the added *angels*.

In town, Claire searched for and found a telephone booth.

The request to call when she landed at the airport or as soon as she reached the home of Mrs. Thompson wasn't fulfilled until nearly a day and a half later. Claire swallowed, muscled up some bravado, and placed the call to her parents. She didn't need an interpreter to tell her they were anxious. Trying not to add to their stress, Claire lied that she was okay and that everything turned out well. She also told them the reason she didn't call when she got there was that it was too late. It seems her mother didn't believe the lie; she begged Claire to come home. But Claire decided, even before she placed the call, to *rough it* out. She hoped to stand firm, no matter how convincing her parents were to come home. She didn't have a solid place to stay, but she felt going back home, even before the vacation period ended, was not the solution. She needed to find her footing. Pity it took going to another country to acknowledge she wasn't standing firm.

Her mom was very supportive and helped her a lot. She was even helpful getting Claire an interview for her work at the hotel. She had asked a friend that was working in the dining room of the hotel to help Claire find a job there, but the only availability was the room attendant position, aka housekeeping. Claire took the *branch* she got; an opportunity to earn some funds, even though her mom wasn't happy with the position. Not only did she survive the sneers of the few that looked down on the position, she kept herself intact. So, she could survive this minor setback here on the island.

When she had accepted the position as room attendant, she went out on a branch; a branch that afforded her the opening to be here now on this island. So she felt it was time to walk out on another branch and test its strength.

They asked how the island and the place were. Some pleasantries were exchanged, and then more questions about the family she was staying with. Not satisfied with her answers, her mom got to the point and asked what was really going on and why was she using a pay phone to call them? Claire said she didn't want to put a long distance call on the people's phone, as they were already being nice to her.

A lying lip is never good. Lots of confessions and prayers tonight.

After more pleadings from her mom, and Claire's reassurance, the automated signaling of more coins needed in the phone slot to continue the conversation sounded. Claire got permission to stay a little longer, but only if everything was okay. Again, she said, things were okay. She promised to come home if things went badly.

Is homelessness considered bad?

Things were already south, but her parents didn't need to know that. She also made a promise to herself to try to make it work out.

She was so deep in thought; it took the consistently busy tone of the phone to remind her the coins had run out and her parents weren't on the line. She noticed Denise and the ladies waiting on her.

She hung the receiver up while wondering if she did the right thing by choosing to stay; it hadn't been a fair trip so far. It was possibly one of the worst anyone would want to experience. Not knowing where your next meal or place of safety is, is worse than bad news. At least you can plan around bad news. But there is nothing you can do about the unknown. She thought of several ways it wouldn't work out to stay, then her reasoning took over and she changed her mind. The proverbial worst is behind you. You have experienced the test and with a helpful angel, have passed.

If homegrown Claire could survive an almost homeless night, what can she not survive?

Those were brave thoughts, but she didn't have time to dwell on them as the ladies had walked on from the phone booth, leaving no other choice but to follow.

Going out and about the town felt good; she liked what she saw, and the journey helped her to forget her troubles for a while. It was a simple walk from where she was staying to the town, no cab or bus fare necessary. Also, she even found she could afford to scrape from her emergency funds for food. The portion was tiny, but it was affordable. Though she was hungry, she saved some of the food for later; maybe for dinner. Maybe she was filled up with worries. Denise offered to buy her more, but she refused. She didn't want to feel like a burden; Denise was already being a good *substitute* host.

The town was small enough for a moderate walker to complete in thirty minutes, if no stops in between, but with the many historical buildings, shopping, and food areas, it would not be possible to keep walking. And as Claire was trying to slow time away from her homeless situation, her legs were like frozen molasses. When she entered a shop or a historical building, she made sure to see every inch of it. It was several hours later before the browsing of the shops ended. Two of the ladies left for another side of the island while Claire, Denise, and the other lady started back toward *home*.

Nothing like a good dose of reality to suck the fun out of a day.

It didn't take long for Claire to be reminded of her sleeping arrangement. It wasn't far from her thoughts, anyway, just wasn't this close to the top of her list. She tried not to worry, but the tour and distractions of the day were wearing off. She had heard nothing from Mrs. Thompson.

While in town she had called the Thompsons' house, but the girl who answered, and who sounded just like the one from the night before, still didn't have a room for her or a message from her mother for Claire.

She wondered if the girl even mentioned anything to her mother. If she was a gambling person, she would back that thought with all her emergency funds; she was pretty sure she would win. Didn't seem they wanted her around; not even as a visitor.

She got the feeling.

It didn't seem she had a future on the island.

She had been there an entire day and night, and she was no closer to understanding why Mrs. Thompson didn't send a message to her, even to say she would be away, or acknowledge her now that she was here.

What was going to happen?

Where would she sleep, or even sit tonight?

There was no guarantee she could rely on Denise's good heart for a second time. The night before, she had only said Claire could stay for the night so she could sort herself out with Mrs. Thompson in the morning. It was now a long way from morning and she was no closer to an answer. All day through the town, Denise had said nothing about her staying another night. She tried not to bring up the subject and was happy Denise didn't ask for an update.

Who supplies an answer to an unasked question? Not Claire.

What's more, she's no mind reader. If Denise was thinking Claire should tell her something, well…

She wasn't sure what her next move was, so she kept quiet on the way back. Denise and her friend chatted about a lot of things, including the way the island was so different from when they first came. They were old friends; it was obvious in their exchange of similar stories, both shared and experienced.

Claire had told Denise she didn't get an encouraging answer from the Thompson house, but said nothing else on the subject.

Denise's simple response, "It will work itself out," stunned her.

Claire renamed Denise the hopeless hopeful; she saw the sun even on rainy days. Therefore, why would Claire put any gloom or make a negative statement about the room? Denise was the one person who had shown her genuine kindness, so she didn't want her to withdraw her hand. If only she could keep her mind, the enemy of her situation, from sabotaging her with reminders of *there's such a thing as overstaying one's welcome.* The mind is a fickle thing; it switches sides quickly.

The Thompson house, which was supposed to be her place of abode, was working its way off the list. She may need to put an ad in the Wanted: In need of room/mate, see me.

It had only been twenty-four hours, but Denise's kindness seemed like an entire year; so, Claire didn't want to rock the proverbial boat. It was best if she made her way up the little avenue she passed earlier. Maybe they were renting.

Her overcrowded thoughts were interrupted by hearing Denise addressing her. "Little K, I'm going to hang with friends later so I won't need the room. You can stay there tonight. Mrs. T is still away, so relax your mind."

Could Denise be any more humane? There are still good people in the world. Brother's [sister's] keeper.

She accepted and thanked her for her generosity. Nothing to think through.

Was there a better offer?

Her only option was taking the room without a bathroom, or a bathroom outside under the skies without a bedroom.

The room wasn't grand, and the knockers didn't make sleep easy. Nevertheless, it was good news. No homelessness.

Rational thinking.

Funny, earlier she put the room down, now the room would put her up.

The irony couldn't be missed. Maybe that's where her heart of gratitude formed.

When they got to the room, Denise and her friend stayed with Claire a little into the early part of the night, then they left for their other friend's house.

Before they left, the trio — Denise, Claire, and Sharon, that's the name of Denise's friend that stayed back — all sat outside under a tree, as the room was too small to accommodate them. The room had simple essentials; a small, single bed, which was taking up most of the space, and a little table with a single chair. That wasn't entertaining space. The room was simply designed to go to bed.

The evening breeze was pleasant and the night light was just right; not dark and eerie as the night before. Perspective will do that for you. Maybe because her mind was in a better place, her energy also lit the way. On the brink of sleeping outside, the place seemed blanketed in darkness and every viper of hell. Tonight, aside from the pesky mosquitoes and sandflies, everything was clearer. And the breeze was strong enough to take with it any extra irritating night-crawlers.

Too bad it can't take the knockers to another street or door.

While the ladies were playing catch-up, Claire tried to take part in the conversation, but she wasn't splendid company. Her mind hadn't settled since she came to the island. Before last night, she would never have considered herself a worrywart, but she had to admit, she had embodied the character and was getting great at it. She thought of every way the night could go wrong and believed it too.

She kept her exchange in the conversation to generic yesses and nos when necessary, so she wasn't missed. And it was an excellent distraction.

It wasn't easy to forget, but she tried to keep her mind away from the past twenty-four-hour's issues. She couldn't help thinking at the fast pace one day changed so much. She felt as if she wasn't *living* back home. She hadn't given thought to where she slept, what she would eat or where she went. Everything, it seemed, she took for granted; just assumed it would be there.

Sadness ate at her inside.

Those everyday but essential things she took for granted were now rare commodities. She was in a bind, a bad one; something she created all on her own by not doing her due diligence and planning this trip from the very beginning to the end of her vacation, if she could call it that. It was over before it started. Now, she was close to penniless; which meant homelessness wasn't far behind. The person she counted on as a support system had gone silent.

Are people led astray because of trusting invitations? Hopefully, few. With any luck, her life was and would be the only test subject.

At least she wouldn't be alone tonight; she could count on the knockers.

And like a clock connected to a power source, as it got darker, the knockers came. Apparently, they didn't get the memo there was a new lodger. Claire secured herself in the room. If there's one thing you can say about a board structure is that there is no secret between the slabs. The knockers whispered, shouted, pleaded, and swore.

She was getting used to the drum playing of the knocks and the shouts and some unfamiliar words; it went with her tears, and pushed her to read her Bible.

She survived the night with not much sleep, but at least she was safe on the inside. The pillow was just as comfy on her head, covering her ears, as when she placed her head on it. There were people on the other side of the door that wanted to get into the room and were practically scraping the door. She was fearful, but it's a good thing fear can immobilize you too. Fear moved her to stay inside.

The next day, Denise brought food with her this time and some splendid news. She must have had a visitation from Claire's Bible reading. After the two days of torture she endured, she felt some good news was *owed* to her. Meeting Denise was like a divine intervention. She had no other explanation for it.

As the road ahead was uncertain, she wanted some better usable news to take her a bit further.

Eager to hear what the good news was, Claire crammed the food away; she barely chewed it, partly from hunger, but mostly to get to the news. However, Denise felt it was too good to rush; so, she took her sweet time. When she was good and ready, finally, Denise told her that she wouldn't need the room at all. And that it was paid up for three more days. Claire was welcome to stay there. And she didn't need to pay her back.

What?!

Best news ever! First day of spring couldn't be greener. Life restored to the emergency pennies ... they will live a few more days.

You can't meet people like Denise every day. Either she had experienced some hardship or similar homeless state to be so compassionate.

Who feels it, knows it.

One must be touched with the feelings of a person's issue to want to do something for them. Obviously, Denise had.

Life had taught her in many lessons that people generally turn up after the time of need has passed. And some will be there in the time of need and miss seeing the need. There's no guarantee they will help you, whether people are early or late.

She hoped not to miss the lesson.

Be present so you can do some good on every occasion.

Denise also said the room was a weekly rental; she mentioned the price, and if Claire wanted to keep it after her lease expired, she would talk to the landlord on Claire's behalf. Seeing she still had three more days to think about it, she was exceedingly happy. What's more, she didn't know anywhere else, and Mrs. Thompson wasn't back.

It was a brilliant plan.

She gave Denise the okay to talk with the landlord before the opportunity disappeared. She didn't know if the rent was any better anywhere else. And even if the room was like a matchbox, at least she and her little bags fit in it. She was happy there was a roof over her head and a place to sleep.

Later she discovered that Ms. Thompson's apartment rental costs exceeded, several times, her emergency funds and the cost of her present room. It was a good thing Claire's sound mind had prevailed and had accepted Denise's offer.

For now, the small room was home. She would make it work.

Claire went with Denise and her friends, and they treated her like she was Denise's daughter. It was a good sanctuary; a safe harbor. Breathing was becoming better.

This was the closest she had come to having a sure foot on land.

The knocking continued.

Maybe it was a good thing the room was paid up, and she was house-sitting, or she would be forced to complain to the landlord, authority, or anyone who would listen. But she considered this was the price of a *freeloader* — er, cough — a free-lodger.

She got some consolation over the next few weeks. The knocking became less frequent. They must have discovered there was a new occupant in the room; gradually, they stopped coming altogether. Before it got to that point, a few times she had seen some young and not so young men wandering in the vicinity. They gave her the eye, as if wondering why she was there and who she was. But they only stared and kept their distance. None were brave enough to approach her; she was okay with that.

She didn't know many people, so she went everywhere about town with the ladies. Even when they weren't buying anything, they walked through the town.

She was getting used to the buildings, streets, shops, and some people. She was amazed how she fit in; it felt like a good place. She liked this little island, unknown to her, before she met Mrs. Thompson. She hoped she had a future on the island.

This rollercoaster called life can be very unpredictable. One minute you are having a great day and in an hour, it sours. Funny how things seem to always take a turn for the worse when things need to get good. Unbeknownst to her, the rollercoaster was about to be derailed as it ran out of tracks.

People can be very harsh, especially when they are judged from the external. Sometimes, you can't see behind the curtain, but most people imagine there is a window there; it is not always so. Curtains have also been placed in front of a wall to give an illusion.

Claire's experience from this point on was nothing compared to being stranded at the gate.

Walking about town was becoming weird; people watched them constantly. Some people stared boldly, but she thought nothing of it. Denise was an exquisite-looking black woman; very tall, five feet nine without heels. Her face, striking, with high cheekbones, showed a mixture of Anglo-Saxon. She always wore her long, sleek, black hair loose down her shoulders; it shined with the morning sun as if brushed every morning and evening. She looked like she was a regular gym member, but it may be from walking into the town every day. So, people staring was nothing new; both genders admired Denise.

However, it was becoming worrisome. It was as if people didn't trust them; the kind of stares you get when you step into a shop with expensive stuff wearing cheap clothing.

The store owners had seen them several times and should be familiar with them by now. They didn't shoplift or eat things before paying, so what gives?

Puzzled, she watched the places they got the stares.

Be careful what you look for, you will find it.

Two weeks later, she learned the true reason of Denise and her friends, and what the stares were about.

She didn't learn it from Denise.

There was an elderly lady that sat outside her store on a plaza they walked by every day; she asked Claire if she was one of the ladies' daughter. She responded no. The lady then asked if Claire knew who the ladies were. Proudly, she said, "Yes, they are my friends."

Apparently, that wasn't an appropriate answer, as it brought her disdainful looks and a mouthful of tsk-tsk! from some of the other ladies nearby.

Strange, those watchers weren't helpful when she needed help, but here they were, helpful to add their paragraph to the long tale told about Denise and her friends.

She got a signed copy from the *bestselling authors;* the ladies by the storefront, *outlaying* the entire fifty chapters of Denise's and friends' biography. The pictures painted weren't the best quality in an association of friendship, and the verbiage wasn't helpful either. It seemed Claire was proudly a part of a ring of *ladies of the night.*

And the storytellers were happy to fill in the blanks for anything she didn't know.

To which Claire said, *"Oh, well."* But finished the statement, *Where were all you bestselling authors when I was homeless?!* in her mind.

She was happy that Denise and her friends had gone into another store; she would be horrified if they caught her giving ear to some *old wives' tales.*

EIGHT

They say, "Show me your friends and I'll show you your future." There's also the, "You are who you hang out with." It's likely there are some truths in those statements, but not every situation is so cut-and-dried. The problem, though, is to know when the statement applies. And even when it applies, people should give a chance for change.

There are countless times when the situation or the person standing before us goes deeper than what we can see. But it's hard to look beyond the surface, especially without facts. And even harder because we sometimes act, then think.

Most publishing companies will agree it's the headline that sells the newspaper or a book. A good headline is like a great commercial; you don't know why you bought the product, you just did. Seems hype is a quicker sale.

When your life or your story is the hottest topic of the day, especially if it's bad, there's no stopping the spread; it goes like wildfire. There's not enough water to douse it. This is how the story goes.

Not long after the discovery of Denise's alleged *night life*, Claire learned the hard lesson of the statement *the company you keep*. She was branded for being in the company of the ladies. That's the simple truth.

People painted her with the same brush; she didn't have a say in the color or choice. Both the blustering tongues of the *mature* ladies around the town and the wandering eyes of the *business* gentlemen painted a distorted image of Claire and hung it, without consent, in the gallery of the streets.

It took some time to notice, and an even longer time to erase the stains. Everywhere she went, she was mocked.

Funny thing, though, the new discovery didn't deter her from hanging out with Denise. Denise helped her that night when she was homeless by her own foolish action; to think she could go to a foreign land without a backup plan, that was Denise. She didn't see her in any other light. She didn't have that kind of information about Denise the night she needed help; there was no brand on her. And if there was a brand, it was the help she extended. Denise was the only person who reached out that night; prostitute or not.

People say *you must not forget your past*. It is also said that the past, the good and the bad, will always be with us. Both viewpoints are true. But what if your past is so tarnished that not even your lifetime of good thereafter gives you a clean slate? It is a sure bet; anyone would wish to forget the past then.

It may be true that you shouldn't erase the past, but it shouldn't drag you backward either. You mustn't let the past be a noose around your neck. Sure, the past may be forgotten for a while or buried beneath layers of nothingness, but it may resurface by a right or wrong trigger. When it does, own it and move on.

Claire wasn't a lady of the night, but as she was branded, if you searched her past and didn't know the full story, you would see it there, and all because she was seen in the company of one or two such persons too many times. You cannot always pick your friends or who will come to your rescue, but if you have been given support when you needed it, you owe it to the universe, and mainly yourself, to pay it forward. Do some good, for goodness' sake.

Because they looked on her as a *lady of the night*, her job options dwindled for genuine work. She was told no one wanted to hire *her kind*. Denise's suspected lifestyle became a noose for her and got tighter when she was seen with Denise or in the company of the other ladies.

She boldly wanted to stick with Denise, but the pressure of unemployment made her wonder if it was time she ventured out on her own. If Denise was a lady of the night, she had never introduced the lifestyle to Claire. She readily provided for Claire anything she lacked.

Venturing out on her own wouldn't be so bad. She knew the lay of the land, so it was unnecessary to depend on Denise's *train* to take her around. What's more, Denise's train had too many stops and was too colorful to be seen on the street. She didn't want to be ungrateful; Denise had been helpful. But she needed to survive. Sure, Denise rescued her from the unknowns.

She shuddered whenever she remembered that night. It wasn't so long ago, but she was trying to put it behind her.

Before she learned of Denise's lifestyle, she didn't think twice about going everywhere with her. She resigned her mind to think of Denise as the same person. She was happy she knew someone else aside from Mrs. Thompson on this island.

The power of choice was hers. She could choose the right path, even in a rough situation. The choice in this situation was to remain friends with Denise. Being around Denise and her lifestyle didn't have to be her reality.

Who knows what would have happened if Denise wasn't a worker of the night and may have been coming off her *night shift?* Not only did Denise find her, she had compassion for her.

Three women entered Claire's life that night; one behind the closed door, the nurse, and Denise. She was offered a place of refuge by the one society deemed undesirable. Denise could have kept on walking; the first lady did. It was her choice to stop and help Claire.

She used to think about the lady that left her at the gate and about Mrs. Thompson, that didn't even consider her plight. But that took a lot of energy to keep them in mind. So, she switched to being grateful for the one that helped her. Perhaps Denise was once a stranger to the island and fell into dark times and didn't want that happening to another person.

Thinking it through, Claire reconsidered her plans to *ditch* Denise's company.

She was without a job and financial help, but that was okay for now. She didn't trade her secluded lifestyle for the mysterious.

Though she wished it wasn't so, some saw her in one light; as fresh meat on the block, down-on-her-luck country girl for predators. That was their perception; she didn't offer any evidence to support such an opinion. She was glad for the temporary reprieve of the absented knockers; they didn't see her a willing participant.

It took some hard work for her to remain friends with Denise and her friends.

Sticking by Denise may have been a terrible choice, but she hadn't compromised herself in any way, so she was free to walk around town with her head still high, and she did. But day by day, as the work option diminished, she was in despair; she smiled in the day, but her tears were her companion at night.

She wasn't a lazy person; work was just avoiding her.

The emergency funds had long since depleted. She ironed a blouse or a skirt for other tenants who maybe were too tired to do their own stuff or pitying her; to help the *little* girl. But it was not nearly enough to do much; the ends couldn't meet.

Frustrated, Claire decided, *enough*. It was time to pack and go back home.

Cleaning hotel rooms wasn't so bad.

Decision made, she told Denise her plan. However, Denise insisted she shouldn't give up. She maintained Claire would find something soon. She should hold on.

Things will get better, Denise kept insisting. And gradually, they did.

Funny, Denise had faith for Claire to find a job, but seemed to have lost it for herself.

Anyway, sure enough, three days later, Claire found work. Correction, works.

Denise had told her about a janitorial company she heard was employing. The job included cleaning offices, banks, and houses, and some babysitting work; no glory front desk, but she could pay her rent and find food. She went and registered herself.

She even landed part-time work selling tickets at night at a theater and waitressing at a diner.

At first, the janitorial company didn't want to give her a job, as they said she was too young. Claire had to prove she was more than capable. Desperation gave her the energy she needed to secure the position. It impressed them at what she could do, which turned out to be a wonderful opportunity for the company; many clients requested Claire, the little girl who does a magnificent job.

Who knows if the hotel room cleaning was a training ground!

She gladly accepted the janitorial work because after Denise had allowed her to stay in the room free for the three days, when those days ended and it was time for her to take over the rent, she came up short by twenty dollars. Denise asked the landlord to give Claire a break until she found work.

The landlord did. He was great at bookkeeping; Claire's name never missed appearing on each page with how much she owed.

During the time leading up to Mrs. Thompson's return, some two weeks later from Claire's arrival on the island, Denise never once asked her if Mrs. Thompson was back or if she knew when she would be back or why she hadn't moved to their house. Luckily, she didn't have to answer. What answer could she give? She didn't know why Mrs. Thompson or her family paid no attention to her. No one asked where she was staying or if she had food. It was as if the invitation was a figment of her imagination.

Claire didn't dwell on the Thompsons either.

Of the many lessons she learned from the ordeal, a few stood out for her: an invitation to come and visit doesn't mean come when you want; not every invitation is real. It's best to make your plans alongside the inviter's; don't just rely on theirs.

Claire was happy with her encounter with Denise; she couldn't repay her even if she had a million dollars, and Denise wouldn't take a penny from her anyway; she had tried many times for the food and back rent.

Denise never left Claire out, and it remained so until Denise left for another country.

As the days turned into weeks, it passed Claire's two weeks' vacation time. Claire kept herself busy with cleaning anything the company sent her to do. She would clean even hours into the night to make up times, as the pay wasn't anything to live by.

It troubled her one day when she realized Denise was upset with her; it wasn't jealousy, she hardly had anything to be jealous over. She didn't want to lose the friendship, though she had some hang-ups. So, she asked Denise what was going on. Denise said

Claire was settling just because she got a job at the janitorial company. She said Claire complained about how big the places she had to clean were for three dollars an hour, for seven hours per day, yet she was still doing it; twenty-one dollars for a building half the size of a football field, and she wasn't looking for changes! She said she'd had enough of Claire's relaxing just because she found a *mop and a bucket*. Her words.

Feeling contrite, she asked Denise what to do. Denise made two requests of her.

One was that she must never find herself in such a position of homelessness, anywhere in the world, again. And two, that she should look for something else to do with her time and brain. Cleaning other people's houses and *whatnot* wasn't for her to make a long-term career. She said if Claire intended to make twenty-one dollars on any job, it should be per hour or working for herself. She had asked Denise what to do, so, she accepted rebuke.

This time, she didn't hesitate. She enrolled in the community college for some night classes; the right track for her young life. As she made the start, things started falling in place. She discovered that attending college wasn't as expensive as she had thought, especially when you have the time to learn. She took two subjects per semester; it was a longer route, but necessary to accomplish something.

Her side jobs earnings covered two subjects.

She had to give up the ticket selling at the theater in order to attend the classes, but she knew, to achieve anything, something's got to give.

It may be odd that throughout the time they spent together, they never proved it that Denise's lifestyle was a lady of the night. She never asked Denise about the kind of work they labeled her with, and Denise mentioned nothing on the subject. There was no mention of another room being rented anywhere either.

Denise was a terrific person who loved to help. She also found out that there was a well-known young man that showed up a lot wherever they were to see Denise; they seemed very close. Maybe that's where her extra dough came from.

As for the knockings on the doors? Well, that has yet to be solved.

One thing for certain, though Denise's work was purportedly as a lady of the night, she was more supportive to Claire than the other woman who crossed her path wearing a *caring uniform;* more than the people in the house behind the closed door, and even more accommodating than the person who invited her to the island, which clearly shows, you shouldn't judge. *But if you must*, don't judge from the outside.

NINE

Saying goodbyes are never easy. Whether it's goodbye to a relationship or a friend moving or even a loved one who's passed on, it can be as straining to see them go as when you first met. It doesn't matter if you knew someone one month or one year, when you are fond of the person, it can be the hardest thing. The worst part is the regret of not letting that person know how they have influenced or affected your life in a positive way.

She achieved her accolades, but regretted losing touch with Denise.

Putting it lightly, she didn't handle Denise's departure quite well. She felt the island had conspired against her with many pitfalls, and considered Denise's leaving was another conspiracy. It felt like she was leaving home all over again and may end up stranded again; the memory didn't bear repeating or reliving. And if Denise wasn't here to rescue her, what would become of her?

She knew long before the actual departure that Denise was leaving, but it still didn't sit well when the time came. She appreciated Denise's sound advice and *motherly* care. Denise added significance in her life and she was quite fond of her. Maybe in the beginning, the fondness was because of what Denise did for her; that act of random kindness was bar none. But over time, her devotion developed into a greater gratitude; a profounder appreciation for Denise's compassionate nature.

She liked that Denise never concerned herself about what people think, particularly of her. She saw that Denise valued people's opinion if it was offered constructively, but whatever you think, negative or positive, Denise says it's on you and you must own up to it.

When she had asked Denise why she was leaving, she said she had outgrown the island. Her exact words. Snooping a little, Denise said when you have done all you can do and then some, it is time to move on to share what you can do with others and to learn from them.

She had never seen Denise teaching anyone needlepoint work, or any other kind of work, for that matter, so she often wondered what skills Denise had to share with others. But it's what it is with some people; the lingo is theirs, and it has more meaning than what the general linguistic person may try to interpret.

Anyhow, Denise later admitted that the real reason she was leaving was that her children called her home.

She had left them when they were eight, ten, and eleven years old, two girls and a boy, in the care of her mother, and had only gone home to see them on the occasional school break or if there was an emergency. She had spent almost all their teenage years away from them; she had been on the island going on ten years.

She shared that her children's father had filed for immigration status in another country for the children and they had approved it, so she was taking them to their father, who had settled down with a wife and wanted his children with them. Denise said it was the best she could do for her children to let them go. After all, she was already living and working in another country. Who knows, maybe that's why Denise showed her so much attention and care; she was like a surrogate daughter for her. She said she planned to stay on a little while in that country and if it worked out, she would make it official; just the same start as what Claire did, and many migrants to a country.

Claire would miss her instructions on *this and that*.

She was a giving person, but Denise showed her how to willingly extend her hand, even when you're not doing so well yourself financially and sometimes emotionally. She also showed her that despite beauty and admiration, you must not be conceited.

Having gone through many rough patches, Claire developed a mental thought on materialistic stuff that served her well over the years: "It's just stuff, and you can't even use it in a turkey." You are free to put your own interpretation on that.

She was glad Denise pushed her on going back to school.

She was really enjoying learning again.

Her favorite subject was economics; it surprised her how much she enjoyed it. It was the subject that got her grounded in her college courses and later, a better career pathway.

Back when she had gone straight to work from high school, Claire thought if she was ever given the opportunity to encourage a person about school, especially someone under the age of eighteen and was still on their parents' education payment, she would tell him or her to learn now while parents or guardians are paying, or pay a hard price later at your own expense. The second time around gets harder on the pocket and time; bills, responsibilities, family, and a lot more get in the mix and add to the pressure of learning.

Seeing this was her *pay to learn* retribution, she made sure she didn't have to do it a third time. She aced the subjects.

The best part of the learning process was the pride she felt in her ability to clean people's houses and offices in the day and study alongside some of those office workers and homeowners in the night. She also felt a bit of competitiveness when the floor-*mopper* could get just as high a grade as the office worker.

She kept her grades going through to the end of her studies and achieved the recognition she wanted. She only wished Denise was there to celebrate with her. Unfortunately, Denise didn't know where she was going to be and for how long, so they fell out of touch. But the thought of Denise, and what she did for her, was never far from her thoughts.

Her time on the island had been secured through a work permit to be legally working on the island. If her school attendance was examined closely, maybe she wasn't supposed to be at the college without a student visa, but that was not an issue back then; she was on a work permit and that was good enough.

In the early part of her job, six months after she arrived on the island, she found that the quietness can get in your head and affect you in a negative way if you don't have the right support system around you.

When she first arrived, praying and talking with the Lord happened quite often, because she knew no other help or person to talk with in the nights. She didn't know of a church building; it wasn't something Denise could point out within walking distance, so most of her time was spent reading the Bible alone. And she was committed to doing it.

And then, she wasn't.

She can't pinpoint when, but little by little, she *relaxed* her stance. Maybe she got tired of hearing the male coworkers' nickname for her; Christian. Some of the guys who made passes at her realized they weren't getting anywhere, so calling her Christian was their defense, it seemed. She didn't mind the average hi and hello, but she wasn't interested in anything serious. She had decided years ago to save herself for the right person. She may have taken some detours to stay the course. It was going well, until she paid a long and hard price for lowering her standard.

She had gotten to where she no longer concerned herself about the Thompsons and whether she would be a part of their life.

Denise had helped her to settle in before she left and had shown her some go-to places for manageable cost on food and rental, if Claire ever wanted a change of scenery. Also, the janitorial company sent her all over the island to work, so she was getting more familiar with the places. She was settling in like it was home. Her parents no longer begged her to come home. Whenever she could, Claire sent some funds home.

On one side, she was finding her way, sometimes to the better side of things. But she was also losing a part of herself in the process. It's difficult for a young person to be alone and remain true; there's always something from the dark side ready to suck a person in if they are not careful. And so, the quiet, Bible-reading, and trying to live a moral life girl swapped that for a different kind of living; nightlife.

The island encourages nightclubs and street dance (called late night sessions then); they were very appealing. Before long, Claire was going on weekends, or whenever she didn't need to go to class or work. It progressed into a habit. She and her Bible didn't meet anymore. She didn't forget God, but pretty soon, their conversation became a *rescue me from this or that, Lord,* when things got bad.

The funny thing was, Claire didn't drink liquor in any form, or smoke, yet she couldn't stay away from the clubs. She formed a compulsion, and the club fed her addiction well; loud music and bright lights. She had never gone to a nightclub back home; never even knew they existed, as she was always at the church before the doors opened and until they were closed. Yet, she was now in them dancing as if something came undone in her. She entered competitions, and won too. Mind you, these weren't ballet dancing either. In fact, the faster the music, the wilder she danced, and guys were noticing; she reaped some unsavory attention.

It appeared that a few of the guys were expecting her to go home with them, and she was defenseless. The situation got so bad one night that she had to pretend she was with another young man to save herself. But he wasn't a savior; he was just as *horny* as the other men and thought she was available for a score. She only extricated herself from him with the help of the guy who later became her first actual relationship—and marked the end of Claire's saving soul for years.

Jolly Claire forgot her parents' favorite idle-time quote, "The devil finds work for idlers." And so before long, "Bad company ruins good morals" (1 Cor. 15:33, English Standard Version.)

After a few weeks of partying with him, it became official; she no longer acted or wanted to be called a Christian. The guy, Harry, was one of the late-night sessions' deejays, so it meant even more merriment for Claire.

Strange, he wasn't a one-girl guy, either. Claire was unaware of it.

Along your journey through life, if you are not grounded in truth, you can be easily swayed. It's imperative to surround yourself with people who encourage you in the right way, or you'll get corrupted and influenced in the wrong way.

Funny how you can survive some difficult things but get *tripped up* by simple things. Claire was not immune to that fault either. She'd spent many years keeping guys at bay; guys she thought were no good and only wanted one thing, yet she let a slippery one in her circle, past her iron barrier. But she was so-called too in love to take notice.

If she should sell the story of her life in a storybook or sequel, it would be a terrible movie, aptly named *When Claire met Harry the Baby Came.*

Tracking backward in her life, she did well in the night college classes. She could have gone on to greener pastures, but she did the opposite of what Denise said; she settled.

When she graduated from the college, she took her certificates to the janitorial company and asked for a position in the office. They told her it was not possible to give her an office job, as her work permit was that of a janitor. Until that time, Claire thought only men were called janitors. Anyhow, the company said it would not be possible to change her job description, per her work permit. She was too naïve to think otherwise, so she continued working with them well over two years as a janitor with a degree in business and office procedures.

Before the clubbing and Harry came on the scene, she had focused a little on one of the owner's sons and he appeared to like her as well, but the limitation of the type of job caused her to doubt it was possible. The relationship didn't develop. She continued to work at the company, but avoided any contact with him. When she didn't move to a cushier position in the office, he didn't seem interested anymore, which put a dent in her self-esteem. Feeling hurt, and other issues, she threw herself into the nightlife and eventually became Harry's girl; temporarily the envy of the other party girls.

As Harry thought nothing was wrong with her job, she didn't bother to seek employment elsewhere. The two were inseparable when she wasn't working. Day by day, he started staying later at her place, even though they weren't physically involved or committing any immoral sin together; strike through the partying. When they went out, he made sure other guys knew she was with him. It was a good feeling to be *owned*. It was a wrong concept, but she felt okay because Harry was well sought after.

The involvement removed the other young man from her head, but he still took up space in her heart. When word got out that she was Harry's girl, the young man tried to talk her out of it, but she refused to give him the time of day. Maybe if she had, she wouldn't be in the *mess* she found herself in not many months down the road.

There's hardly one person who hasn't had a few *maybes* in their life; she had several. Her life was filled with working, partying, and Harry, and that was okay by her. But it didn't seem enough for him. He was restless, yet he told her she was too free, having too much time to party.

According to him, *after the fact*, she should have more responsibility; like a baby.

Can you imagine a guy that plays music all night and sleeps most of the day saying she needs more responsibility? That should have been her retort, or she should have seen the red flag, but Claire wasn't thinking clearly. She was gratified to be Harry's girl and thought it was a badge of honor. What's more, she wasn't seeing any better prospects.

And she was old enough to start a family.

She went from not sleeping together to one night of giving in. One night, she was *in love* and gave in. And that's all it took; one night, one time. It was a painful night, and as she was in no hurry to repeat it, they kept their distance. Imagine her surprise when she found a life growing within her.

She also found out later that her constant dependency on Denise was transferred to Harry. Instead of looking for a godly influencer, she idolized someone who wasn't interested in doing church. And as her faith wasn't as grounded as she thought, she was easy prey.

At the early stage of the pregnancy; around three months later, the thrill of Harry and Claire completely wore off. Her eyes opened. She couldn't go back to the clubs.

Was this the life she thought for herself, literally barefooted and pregnant? Imagine how mortified she was when he said he didn't want another child. His words.

Another child.

She learned, late, that she was one of several baby mamas.

He had been crashing at her place regularly because she demanded nothing of him; no maintenance, and her legs were too closed. He was pursuing her innocence, and she was too innocent to see.

What was she thinking allowing him to sleep there even when they weren't intimately involved? Clearly, she wasn't thinking. There's an intoxicating feeling when your desire is near; your wit or wise-mindedness take second chair.

When she discovered her pregnant state, a doctor got the first call. She wanted to relieve herself of the burden. She didn't know how to tell her parents or the company she worked at. Both made demanding rules to live by where pregnancy was concerned.

She knew how let down her parents would feel.

Before the pregnancy, she had gone home for visits a few times and her parents were happy with the way she was keeping herself in check; they didn't know about the clubbing, but they knew she didn't make it out to church as often as they would like. But they were still grateful their daughter made it back to them in a sound mind and body.

While some women felt overjoyed and special about their pregnancy, Claire felt suffocated and alienated.

She had no one to talk to or turn to. Harry took the escape clause and never looked back.

Of her mother's many *commandments*, there was one about being pregnant and unmarried: "None of you girls get pregnant before you get married and think you can come back home." That *commandment* had been instilled in her even before her monthly cycle. Her parents were big believers in the *marriage then child* system. So even to be knocked up at the ripe age of over twenty-two was still a no-no. She was happy she made it through her teen years unpregnant, but she was unmarried, and that was a big taboo with her parents.

Looking back, there were so many lessons she gathered on the rocky road she found herself. There may have been a lot more she learned, but hardly anyone in a rough patch pays attention to lessons.

One important thing she remembered and wished to highlight is that sometimes parents should revisit the rules they made when the child was younger. And as the child gets older, the parents could tweak those rules. They could let the child know how proud they were of them they are now past the precarious childhood stage. Let the child know how proud they are of their achievements; don't just assume the child knows. The knowing could make a whole lot of difference for a struggling child.

She found out a little late that she had more than help; she just didn't know she had them. Her alienation was her own doing, and her suffocated feeling was part of life.

While she was trying to figure out what to do with her life, life was busy figuring out what to do with her, and it didn't seem like a good plan.

She was unprepared.

Not only was she homeless, she was alone and pregnant.

Many times when her mind flashed back to that experience, she regretted not seeking help before it was too late.

Instead of being homeless and raising a child on her own—and failing miserably at it—she could've gone home to get support. But as she had hidden her condition from her parents, she learned late that they no longer held the rigid rule of the unmarried and pregnant daughter in their home.

But before she got to the *good* street life, her business made it home to her parents before she did.

Small villages do get the word around.

When she was five months pregnant, and still hadn't worked up the courage to let her parents know, the news spread and her parents heard. They weren't pleased at what happened to her or how they got the news, but they were forgiving, and told her she could come home when she was ready. Fourteen months later, she took the baby home so she could return to work. She also took home her fiancé.

Our life can flash before us on a billboard or in the drop of a tear, but one never knows how an *if I had known* moment would come about. Many of us lived the *if I had known* from some bad experiences, but it can always be viewed from some not so bad ones as well.

Going to the island from a church life environment, she thought she had it made. She had spent a good number of years in church, but perhaps for a good number of years, the Church wasn't in her.

In her life, which may not be so different from others, she had suffered and endured some setbacks, but as former World No. 1 professional tennis player Billie Jean King says, "Pressure is a privilege." Claire welcomed now each setback with an *I will get through this* bravado. Not many faced pressure, so she was privileged.

When we are in the midst of something, we don't see it that way, and then we have a lot of *if only I had known.* Her if only I had known came after the baby, a bad situation, but it turned out for good. She was thankful she didn't go any further with the baby's father or the appointment to see the abortion doctor. The road ahead looked bumpy, but she wouldn't be the first person — or the last — to reset their dreams after a setback.

Telling her workplace about her pregnancy was hard. She was sure they would let her go or stop her at six and a half to seven months. She didn't have enough money saved for a week without work, much less two and a half months and with a baby. So she *lied* at five months that she was three months pregnant; her stomach was a tiny bump, so she got away with it. At nine months, when she was ready to deliver the child, the company gave her time off, thinking she was seven months.

She apologized for the deception.

The experience taught her that though you can't predict where the future will take you, you have a hand in what you do before you get there.

Though cesarean delivery, she pushed her body to heal so she could return to work a month and a half later. The company took her back. She stayed there six months and she finally got the nerve to apply for other positions in other companies; it paid off.

Claire believes no *fairy tale* ending is true. The girl doesn't always get the guy. The baby doesn't always make it past the abortion clinic. The ring doesn't always make it onto the ring finger. But despite her mishaps, she sometimes adopted the rosy-glass view to see a happier future, even after her slips.

Every day she works towards that end.

TEN

When Claire left her country, it was for a two-week vacation, but ultimately it turned into months, and later years, with many job changes and a husband and two children.

The in-between years saw her pregnant, unmarried, and then married and pregnant. Her life wasn't as *sparsely* colored as this story mentions; you were spared the gruesomeness to get to the other side of a good day.

But for your interest, some lines were said in the directness of how it happened, outside of her disappointment with the way her invitation worked out. Inside that invitation was a whole lot of good. She met and married her *foreign* suitor, a native of the island. They have been married nearly three decades, with two children and one grandchild.

Her work timeline has taken her from the hotel and janitorial cleaning jobs to working as a cashier and later as a supervisor at a major supermarket. She had also worked as an administrative assistant and later as a personal secretary to a loan officer in one of the biggest banks there. She even worked as a manager of a major hotel. And most importantly, owning several businesses on that same island that didn't welcome her on her first day.

These scenes played out for her because she went out on a limb and acquired some skills while barely balancing her life. She still remembers the path that took her to those accomplishments; her meeting with a lady when she worked as a room cleaner in a hotel.

Outside of the homelessness mentioned in the story, she experienced these three other times, once when fire consumed everything she owned. She was penniless many times, and one too many times compromised, but it never broke her and never will.

She remained grateful for the night she had no room in Mrs. Thompson's *inn*, which led her to a stranger who played the Good Samaritan, even if she was a lady of the night.

Funny, when Mrs. Thompson eventually returned to the island two weeks later, Claire went to visit her. She hadn't been keeping in touch with the children because four times she had contacted them and was unsuccessful, so she had stopped calling the house or asking if Mrs. Thompson asked after her.

If it wasn't for Denise, she may never have found out that Mrs. Thompson had returned.

Sitting across from the lady who, without reservation, or so Claire thought, had invited her to visit her island, Claire felt like they were strangers. The atmosphere was awkward. Perhaps neither knew what to expect, given what had happened. Claire felt uncomfortable sitting inside the hallway on an invitation to come in, yet she couldn't get past the front door when she needed it most.

She wasn't bitter. It worked out great; she met Denise. But she still locked the hurt in her heart of being locked out of the house in the strange land.

It was just after lunchtime, but there was no presence of a meal or drink for her visit. The host never offered her anything to drink, not even a glass of water.

Mrs. Thompson didn't ask her why she wasn't staying at her home as per the original plan. She never asked where she was staying. She didn't offer any information about her *unexpected* trip to the USA. She never said whether she knew that Claire was on the island all this time. She never mentioned the reason the children didn't have an option for where Claire should stay. The discussed hotel front desk clerk job never came up either.

Claire never told her she knew her real job at the hotel was a room cleaner, not the front desk supervisor, as she claimed. Neither did Claire tell her what happened the night she arrived on the island and the way they treated her. She didn't tell her where she was staying or who helped her with the room. Mrs. Thompson, it seemed, wasn't interested in how she was getting along. Claire didn't mention she got a job either. She didn't know if it would make any difference to dredge up the past, even if it was only two weeks ago; she couldn't go back, only forward.

As she sat across from Mrs. Thompson, she thought how mortified she would feel if she had done this to someone. No amount of remorse could make up for putting someone through that experience.

The room was extremely quiet, which was unusual. Their past conversations were animated and cheerful; they chatted away like old friends. Now, the conversation was like someone asking about the weather or an interview.

Mrs. Thompson asked her what she had seen of the island so far and what she thought. Claire said everything was fine. She was getting good at lying. Nothing to brag about, but what else is there to say? Did she need to tell her how she found the house? Did she need to tell her that Denise gave her a place to stay? Did she owe her anything for the invitation? Apparently, they had nothing to talk about.

No apologies were offered.

Neither seemed to hold the other accountable for that night's mishap.

The only personal question between them was when Mrs. Thompson asked her if Claire was extending her two-week break. Claire's response was an unofficial, who knows. And that was being honest.

Who knows what tomorrow will bring?

If today was anything to go by, tomorrow might be worse; it is the day after.

Who knows if she wants to divulge her plans?

What good did sharing her plan do for her when she set out for the island? No one picked her up from the airport or put her up for the night. Just the kindness of a stranger was why she was sitting there.

Who knows why they were here making small talk? Were they in front of a psychotherapist? Did they need a mediator?

Who knows what the island holds for Claire; she was safe one day and in minutes could have been a missing person.

So, Mrs. Thompson, who knows?

This wasn't the journey she set out on, but it was the journey that found her. She accepted the privilege and is living by it. There are many lessons to be learned from someone else's experience.

Claire didn't have a compass or memo whether her life was going to be on this road, but she has learned to adapt.

We can never be too high not to accept a branch, even from ones we consider the lowest. We should try not to look down on anyone, as their state might be ours the next day. As the earth spins on its axis, so does our situation.

Denise could have easily passed her that night, left her at the gate, just like the other lady did. Denise could've kept her business room and carry on; it was allegedly her livelihood, and maybe her daily bread. She sacrificed herself for a stranger.

Who knows; maybe she was an answer to a prayer Denise prayed to be rid of her lifestyle. Maybe a God wink moment.

A rocky start doesn't have to be a bad ending. There are opportunities in almost every situation. You don't have to close yourself off because of a setback or a turnaround on your journey.

Claire has long since forgiven herself for traveling without a secured plan.

If everything had worked out as planned for Claire; two weeks' vacation at Mrs. Thompson's, maybe her life would have been different. Maybe she might still be working as a housekeeper. Maybe she mightn't have traveled further than Mrs. Thompson's island. Maybe she wouldn't have met her remarkable husband and have her businesses.

She embraces the thought that not every disappointment is bad.

Not every derailment means a missed destination.

In the end, it worked out for her.

Like Joseph in the Bible, she could also say, "What the devil meant for bad, God turned it around for good" (Gen. 50:20).

We all have enough opportunities in the present, and will have in our future, to pay forward good deeds to others because of what we have been saved from or given in our past. Whenever you can, you must **put some good in your day** for it to be a *good morning, good afternoon, good evening, and a good night.*

You should know, your life is not over just because of one disappointment, one wrong turn, or if a lady of the night is your only help. You are not alone.

Since that island visit, Claire has traveled as far as Greece and Israel, and to over fifty other countries; in Europe, England, and the Caribbean, and several states in the USA and provinces in Canada. Though she didn't become an air hostess, traveling remains her passion.

After some roundabout turns, Claire recommitted her life to God and is an active member of the body of Christ.

And talk about the past coming back to haunt you. Wouldn't you know it, the nurse lady serves along with her in the same church now and they are good friends! She wrestled with the thought, several times, to ask the lady if she was a Christian from back then, that dreaded night, but has resisted. If the lady was a Christian, she might have struggled with the thought of how she left that young girl at the gate. No sense in guilting her further. But one thing is certain, if the lady was calling herself a Christian then, she may have missed the Christ-like nature; "The least you do for others..."

It's all behind her now, in the past where it belongs.

Several years later, she came across the helper that worked at Mrs. Thompson's during the time; she was at the house that night and had begged the girls to let Claire in and they ignored her. She also said when she had mentioned to Mrs. "T" how a young girl turned up a few nights ago looking for her, but the children didn't let her stay at the house, Mrs. "T" had said she knew who it was, but she didn't expect she was going to take her up on her offer to come over to the island.

Makes one wonder what is an invitation?

According to the Oxford dictionary, an invitation is "a **written or verbal request inviting someone to go somewhere** or to do something." It also says, "A situation or action that tempts someone to do something or makes a particular outcome likely." It was clearly a verbal request to go somewhere she got from Mrs. Thompson.

But if by inviting someone you don't want to take you up on your offer is not clear enough, perhaps you should add some conditions. Criteria such as, one: I am inviting you, but that doesn't mean you should take me up on the offer. Two: saying you can come any time doesn't mean you should show up when you feel like it. Three: if you are ever in the area, look me up, but first let me know you are coming to the area. Four: if you don't take me up on the invitation right now, the offer expires. With such criteria, at least the invitee would *think and think* some more before taking you up on the offer.

What Claire finds intriguing is that her parents were hesitant to let her go abroad, yet her inviter readily agreed for her to come. She had said she was excited about her involvement in Claire's first trip abroad. Looking back, Claire realized that Mrs. Thompson fulfilled her role; she was *involved* in *Claire's first trip abroad*. Maybe she wasn't supposed to do anything beyond that.

Oh well.

Winston Churchill says, "Never waste a crisis." Was she in one? Of course. She likes to think Denise rescued her that night, as she rescued Denise. Crisis unwasted.

She also learned that it is important to have influential and beneficial support.

Surrounding yourself with good people doesn't mean you will be good. But you stand a better chance of getting better. A believer can become discouraged and corrupted and lose hope when they encounter people who are not living up to the faith. A nascent journey is something to look forward to. Along the journey — and Claire is still journeying — she discovered that the world is much bigger than her *comfort* zone.

It is Claire's hope that her experience and subsequent overcomer state encourages someone to push past the darkness that may surround their situation.

Some encouraging and uplifting quotes to take on your journey.

No matter where you are on your journey, you can have a new beginning.

The journey you are on may not be the one you have chosen, but you can adjust your sails along the way to get to where you want to be.

You may not control the bumps on the road, but you can learn to enjoy the journey.

If you haven't figured it out, take note that tolerance is necessary on any journey. You may meet people that will not be your ideal choice of friends or acquaintances, but if you are ever in a bind, hopefully you will come away from that more welcoming of all people.

We shall not cease from exploration. And the end of all our exploring will be to arrive where we started and know the place for the first time.

                                        ~ T.S. Eliot

**Some Published Books
by the Author**

The Power to Persevere
A Loggerhead Tale
Before Evil Walks
The Cayman Islands Trivia
Three Parrots On A Limb
The Cayman Islands A-Z
Jel Jel the Melting Jellyfish
The Lucky Crab
A Fun Way to Connect with Bible Stories
Unlocking the Prayer of Jabez

Coming in 2021
Daily Benefits
Infiltrate
Netted Faith
The Son of a King in a Borrowed Tomb
My Three Little Dots on the Big World Map

www.ingramcontent.com/pod-product-compliance
Lightning Source LLC
Chambersburg PA
CBHW060355180626
46817CB00008B/3020